J. A. O'Brien began work with Irish Railways after leaving school but went to college at twenty to qualify in theoretical radio and electronics. He returned to Ireland after a job as a stock clerk in Smithfield to work for Eircom for twenty-eight years.

FOUL DEATH

DI Sally Speckle gets a phone call from a man who calls himself Fred telling her that he has left a birthday present for her at the Old Mill. The call makes no sense, but it unnerves her, particularly as the call is from a payphone in Loston Mental Hospital. Her present is the battered body of a faceless young woman. Then there is a second body and Speckle and her team realise they are dealing with a possible serial killer. Who will keep a cool head and save Fred's next victim, unmask the killer and solve the case?

Books by J. A. O'Brien
Published by The House of Ulverscroft:

PICK UP
OLD BONES
REMAINS FOUND

J. A. O'BRIEN

FOUL DEATH

Complete and Unabridged

ULVERSCROFT
Leicester

First published in Great Britain in 2009 by
Robert Hale Limited
London

First Large Print Edition
published 2010
by arrangement with
Robert Hale Limited
London

British Library CIP Data

O'Brien, J. A. (James A.)
Foul death.
1. Policewomen- -Fiction.
2. Serial murder investigation- -Fiction.
3. Young women- -Crimes against- -Fiction.
4. Detective and mystery stories. 5. Large type books.
I. Title
823.9'2–dc22

ISBN 978–1–44480–098–2

Published by
F. A. Thorpe (Publishing)
Anstey, Leicestershire

Set by Words & Graphics Ltd.
Anstey, Leicestershire
Printed and bound in Great Britain by
T. J. International Ltd., Padstow, Cornwall

This book is printed on acid-free paper

PROLOGUE

The floorboard creaked. The intruder paused. Listened. Waited. The house remained per- fectly still, except for the wind that squeezed in, as wind does, and sighed along the hall with the wearines of an old man close to death. The house was in total darkness, the way he liked it. Of his previous six visits, two had been nocturnal. He knew every inch of the house.

The name of the woman he had come to murder was Claire Shaw.

Green eyes looked at him through the bannisters on the landing above him. Cromwell was the cat's name and he liked, of all things, chocolate, which his mistress treated him to twice a week on Wednesdays and Sundays.

The man knew all there was to know about Claire Shaw.

She was twenty-nine years old. A natural blonde. She took size four shoes, except in the summer when her feet became swollen and she wore size four and a half. She liked red wine, even with fish, and she hated gin because it made her feel queasy. She had

1

three A levels, and her favourite subject at school had been history, particularly the Tudor period, and within that period Anne Boleyn whom, she would argue, was treated rather unfairly by Henry who was, it seemed, ready to listen to any accusation against her.

It was Claire's interest in the Tudor period which had given the cat its name. Cromwell, she had confided, was a man she could have fancied had she been around back then. She liked the colour red best, and always managed in every outfit to include it somewhere. She was single, but was having an affair with a married man whose name was Alistair, a stockbroker full of his own importance. He would never leave his wife for Claire. Sarah Worth was very beautiful and very rich in her own right, and if her beauty did not win out with Worth, her money certainly would.

He went into the sitting-room to collect the murder weapon he had chosen on a previous secret visit to the house, a heavy poker. Then he went upstairs with a ghostly stealth to the landing above and Shaw's bedroom. Cromwell came to rub against him. He put the poker under his arm to allow him to pick up the cat in his gloved hands. He tickled the tom under the chin, and then twisted its neck without qualm, not wanting to risk his running ahead when he opened the bedroom door. He eased open the door on hinges he had oiled on a previous visit, just in case, and stood shocked. Claire Shaw was not there. In his shock, he almost missed the click of the bathroom light switch next door to the bedroom. His cocky casualness had almost been his undoing. The bathroom door began to open. Now that she was wide awake, to avoid any possibility of a fight back, he would have to strike swiftly. He would have preferred, had she been asleep, to wake her for the second before he killed her, to send her winging into eternity knowing who her killer had been; knowing it was him, her surprise frozen in her dead eyes. It angered him now that that would not be possible. He raised the poker, ready to swipe when Claire Shaw appeared. In a red haze of rage, he smashed her face with the first awful blow. She staggered back into the bathroom, blood gushed and spilled over her pristine white dressing-gown like a plague spreading unhindered. It splashed over the name 'Claire' on her left breast. Another blow, even more forceful than the first totally destructive strike that had caved in the right side of her face, smashed her nose and the left side of her face. She crashed to the bathroom floor, blood spewing from her shattered head. The soggy sound of flesh and bone disintegrating drove him on in a bloodlust fury.

Blow!

Blow!!

Blow!!!

He had never thought that murder would make him so sexually aroused. Spent, he sat on the floor next to the dead, faceless woman. A slow grin began on his mouth that matured into fullblown laughter, manic in its intensity. His laughter haunted the still house.

He had killed his first victim for Detective Inspector Sally Speckle, the first in what he hoped would be a long line of victims.

1

DI Sally Speckle, hand under her chin, looked a touch gloomily at the desk calendar on the breakfast counter. The month showing on the calendar was September. A red cross marked the sixteenth — the sign Virgo. She was thirty years old. And, like everyone else on their birthday, she had mixed emotions. She mused on things that might have happened; or things which had happened, for good or bad; things she might have done differently, or not have done at all. She recalled decisions she had taken, and mistakes she had made. Good times, sad times, bad times, and times that could not be categorized; the outcomes of which could not as yet be assessed with any degree of plus or minus — a work in progress, one might say. And as always, memories. Of the day her father walked out; of the day her gay brother had died of AIDS and the long months of worry as his health failed and his death had become inevitable. Her father had briefly returned, not that she cared either way by then. After the funeral she had said goodbye to him, much to his relief, she reckoned. The thing was that he had never given a reason to her why he had left, only an assurance that it was not for another woman. Harry Speckle had just seemed to grow tired of his family, which was the most hurtful thing of all.

The phone rang.

'Speckle.'

She winced at sounding so official, but she had answered so many times as a police officer, she found it difficult to sound personal. The public expected their police officers to sound as though they were capable of solving their problems, not an agony aunt service.

'Happy birthday, ma'am,' said Andy Lukeson banteringly.

'Thank you, DS Lukeson,' she replied, with a gaiety she was far from feeling.

'You sound chirpy for forty,' he teased, his laughter cheeky.

'Forty is a great year. And, in the not too distant future you should be in a position to verify the same, Andy.'

'Ouch!'

'And less of the *ma'am*.'

'Ready for your chat with the new broom, then?' he enquired.

The new broom being the recently appointed Assistant Chief Constable Alice Mulgrave, who was on what she termed a

6

familiarization tour, vetting being too emotive a description of her visits to the stations which had come under her jurisdiction. The chat to which Lukeson had referred was a meeting with Chief Superintendent Frank 'Sermon' Doyle and Mulgrave.

'We all have to be on our best behaviour,' Doyle had warned. 'Not only will Alice Mulgrave be paying us a visit, she is also taking up residence here in Loston until she decides on a more permanent base, hopefully not in Loston,' he had added glumly.

'As ready as I'll ever be, Andy. Pity Jack Lucas didn't get the job. One of our own. The devil you know, and all that.'

'Drink after work?'

'That would be lovely.'

'I'll pick you up in ten minutes,' Lukeson said matter-of-factly.

'No need. I have the Punto back; it was a dodgy water pump.'

'About time you scrapped that car, isn't it?'

'Why? It's given me ten years' good service.'

'Ten years. That's the point.'

'The Punto is like an old friend, Andy. And old friends are to be cherished. And anyway, I would be changing for another Punto. Fiat make great cars; it's people like me who wreck them.'

'See you later, then. Bye.'

She picked up the cup of coffee on the breakfast counter and sipped it reflectively. The phone rang again. This time she replied with a bouncy, 'Hi!'

A payphone.

'And how is the birthday girl?' the man said. 'Full of the joys it seems.'

'Who is this?' she asked, unable to stop the cold finger that ran along her spine, for which there was no reason that she could fathom.

'Like the new birthday hairdo,' he said.

Sally Speckle tensed.

'Those blonde highlights are what our American friends would call a knockout.'

'Who is this?' she demanded to know.

'So uptight, and on your birthday, too, Inspector,' he said. 'Of course I suppose you have your worries. Thirty. Bio-clock running. Tough, that. Maybe you should screw Lukeson and get it over with. God knows you want to.'

She looked around for something to jot down the number of the payphone showing on the caller display. But, as always, like a policeman, there is never a biro around when you need one. Not that it would do much good. He had called her Inspector, so he was hardly likely to hang about once he had finished the call to wait for the police to

8

arrive. She turned out the sugar bowl onto the breakfast counter and wrote the calling number in the sugar, giving herself credit for her quick-wittedness.

'Who are you?' she demanded to know.

'I'm Fred. And, it being your birthday, I've left a birthday present for you at the Old Mill.'

He hung up.

She hit the redial button. No reply. Probably a street kiosk. No one ever answered a ringing public phone. She was about to hang up when a man answered. Not the same voice; this one was rougher.

'Can you tell me where that phone is, please?'

'Don't ya know where you're callin'?'

'It was just a number left for me to call back,' Speckle lied.

'The hospital.'

'Loston General Hospital?'

'No. Loston Mental Hospital.'

The shiver along her spine when the man had phoned was back, but chillier.

'Where exactly is the phone located in the hospital?'

'Reception.'

'Did you see a man use that phone just now?'

'No. I was just passin' and picked it up.' His tone of voice said that he wished he had not.

'And you are?'

'What's that got to do with the price of eggs, eh?'

Speckle did not press him.

'Is there another man in reception right now?'

'Shooter's hangin' abou'.'

'Shooter?'

'As in revolver. Works here at the hospital. A musician — Albert Hall kind. Part of some arty-farty music-therapy lark. All a lot of old bollocks, thinkin' that slappin' on a piano will do anythin' for a nutter, ain't it?'

'Would you ask Mr Shooter to come to the phone?'

Speckle was sure that she'd recognize the man's voice if she heard it again so soon after.

'Look, I ain't got no time to mess abou',' the man complained. 'I'm a bloody cleaner, not a messenger.'

'It's very important that I speak to him.'

The phone went dead.

Speckle phoned back, but the number went unanswered.

★ ★ ★

'Loston Mental Hospital,' said a cheery female voice a couple of minutes later — much too upbeat for a mental facility,

Sally thought — when she phoned reception. The receptionist's greeting was more appropriate to a five-star hotel or a travel agent than a mental hospital. 'Kate speaking. How may I help you?'

'My name is Detective Inspector Sally Speckle of Loston CID.'

'What's happened? Father hasn't been making a nuisance of himself, has he?' Before Speckle could reassure the receptionist that, to her knowledge he had not, she went on apace: 'He doesn't mean any harm. He's just getting a bit forgetful and sometimes gets frustrated because he can't remember things.'

'I'm not calling about your father,' Speckle said. 'I was speaking to a man on the payphone in reception just now.'

'That'll be Larry.'

'Larry?'

'Brite. Not bright as in spark. B-R-I-T-E. He works for the contract cleaners. He's gone now.' Another phone rang. 'Back in a mo,' she sang out.

The haunting music of Acker Bilk's 'Stranger on the Shore' came on the line and it brought back bitter-sweet memories for Speckle. She recalled how her father had bought a clarinet, promising to play Mum to sleep every night with 'Stranger on the Shore' as soon as he learned to play, but like most things, Harry Speckle had soon tired of his ambition, and the clarinet had ended up on top of the bedroom wardrobe gathering dust. When he left, Mum had binned it.

'That's all I need. Another reminder of your father's broken promises,' she had said bitterly, when Sally Speckle had asked.

Kate flashed back on line, not a tenth as cheery as she had been. 'It's all go here, and I'm on my own. Shirley is off with flu. Look, Larry hasn't been . . . ?'

'Hasn't been what?' Speckle prompted, when the receptionist tapered off.

'You being a police officer, and all.' Speckle waited. 'Well, one of those calls . . . to women. Don't you have that on your files? Lucky he didn't go to prison. I reckon he deserved more than a suspended sentence, even if it was a first offence.'

So Larry Brite had form for making nasty calls to women. Interesting. Very interesting indeed.

'Is Mr Shooter there?'

'Mr Shooter?' Kate asked, sounding somewhat in awe.

'Yes. Mr Brite said he was.'

'He had no call doing that. Mr Shooter's such a nice man.' The subtext being that Larry Brite was not a nice man. 'He was, but he's gone. He'll be with Dr Daniels now.'

'Did Mr Shooter use the payphone?'

'Mr Shooter use a payphone?' Obviously the idea was daft. 'Mr Shooter would never use a public phone. He has this thing about germs; a phobia. Used the phone here at reception once, and I thought he'd wear it out cleaning it with his handkerchief. Oh, no, a public phone would be the last thing Mr Shooter would use.'

'Did you see anyone using the payphone, Kate?'

'No. It was very busy and, of course, it's almost impossible to see the payphone from the desk because it's in a nook.'

'I'll need Mr Shooter's address.'

Brite's she could obviously get off the database.

'I couldn't give you that. Hospital policy.'

'This is a police inquiry,' Speckle said, with official pomposity.

'Crikey. I'll have to give you our Mr Thomas, then.'

The bleep of an extension phone came on the line. There was a silent pause, no doubt while the receptionist explained the nature of the call and caller.

'Thomas speaking,' came the brusque reply, a moment later. 'Mr Shooter is a very private person, Inspector Speckle. You do understand that being the kind of hospital we are, we have to be cautious.'

'Of course I do, Mr Thomas.'

'You wouldn't mind awfully if I checked with Loston Police that you are who you say you are, Inspector?'

'A sensible precaution, Mr Thomas.'

'If I could have the number you're calling from, I'll phone you back as soon as possible.'

Sally Speckle gave him her phone number, with the suggestion that he should speak to CS Doyle. While waiting for Thomas to call back, Speckle gave her mind over to the man who had phoned her — the creepy Fred. He knew that she had had her hair done. He knew it was her birthday. And he knew her unlisted phone number. She let her mind go back to the previous evening. She had left the hairdresser at 5.30, had done some shopping in a nearby supermarket. She had then called into the newsagent near her house to order a back number of a magazine, and had then gone directly home. She tried to recall any man who might have taken an interest in her, but to no avail.

Looking at nothing in particular, Sally Speckle suddenly went rigid. And the cause for her alarm was the coffee stained mug on the draining-board. She was meticulous about washing-up (fussy was not a word she liked, but it was a word that someone might

14

use to describe her preoccupation with neatness), and she would never have left a mug on the draining-board, everything in its proper place. The brown ring at the bottom of the mug suggested that the mug had been washed and left to dry of its own accord. Now other things came to mind. The cushions on the sofa; she always kept them fluffed up. And now . . . She hurried to the sitting-room. Yes, she had been right. The centre cushion of three was flattened. Someone had sat against it. She always sat in the left corner of the sofa to watch telly, and never failed to fluff the cushion when she got up. Her gaze shot to the figurine on the mantel, always dead centre, the Spanish dancing lady was now more to the right of centre. Her breath caught in her throat.

Someone had been in the house!

And that explained how Fred had got her unlisted number. When she had changed from her flat to a house it meant a change of telephone number, and the technician who had connected the new phone had put her new number on the phone until she got used to it. 'You'd be surprised how easy it is to forget a new number. Just take it off when you've got it in your head.'

There were no signs of forced entry, but then an expert intruder would leave no sign.

Speckle had a mental image of the man calling himself Fred, making himself at home, drinking coffee from that displaced mug, watching telly while he did so.

The police officer in Sally Speckle took over. The mug had probably been washed, so fingerprints and DNA would likely be lost, but one never knew. She'd have them bagged anyway. Of course any DNA or fingerprints would only be of use if Fred had a record (Brite came to mind). Or, if he did not have form, only when he was caught. The rough, mixed fibre cushion, should be a good collector of hairs and fibres that might indicate an occupation or profession, or perhaps social class based on the quality of the material, or, if the garment could be traced back to a store, the area in which it was located might point the finger at someone. She went and checked every inch of the house, filled with doubts about having moved from a flat to a house — houses were easier to break into.

It worried her that if the caller thought her new hairdo had been a knockout, his interest in her was probably sexual. He had mentioned leaving a present for her at an old mill. What present? What old mill?

DI Sally Speckle's thoughts became dark.

The phone rang, sending her nerves jangling.

'Inspector Speckle?'

'Mr Thomas, good of you to call back so promptly.'

'Rupert Shooter's address is 3 Allworth Avenue, Inspector.' Allworth Avenue. A location that had featured prominently in her first murder investigation.[1] 'I do hope that Mr Shooter will not be too odd,' Thomas fretted. 'He is of an artistic temperament and easily upset.'

'I'll take great care, Mr Thomas. Thank you. Do you have CCTV in the reception area?'

'Yes. Every nook and cranny, actually. A bit unnerving sometimes to have one's every move watched, don't you think?'

'I'd like to view the footage, Mr Thomas.'

'You mean this morning's footage?'

'Yes.'

'Sorry. That's not possible. There isn't any footage, you see. Normally we would have, from every possible angle, but at present the system is being upgraded and is out of action, Inspector.'

'Is that so,' Speckle said, with interest.

With CCTV out of action, it suggested that the payphone user was in the know: someone on the staff? Or someone delivering a service

---

[1] See *Pick Up*

to the hospital, perhaps? Someone like Brite or Shooter, maybe?

'It was pretty obsolete. The new system will give us very high definition, rather than the grainy footage the old system provided,' Thomas boasted.

'All staff would have been informed that the CCTV was temproraily out of use, would they, Mr Thomas?'

'Yes, Inspector. For security reasons they would have to be a bit more vigilant with the CCTV system not functioning.'

'And other staff, such as cleaners and others on contract?'

'I suppose so. They wouldn't have been informed officially, but, of course, working in the hospital they would have heard, I imagine.'

'Thank you for your help, Mr Thomas.'

Speckle phoned Lukeson.

'Andy, what do you know about old mills in or near Loston?'

'There's only one. An old textile mill on Buxton Street. Been idle for an age. Lost out to cheap imports. Why?'

'I think there's a body there, Andy,' DI Sally Speckle said sombrely.

2

'What's this about a body, then?' Lukeson asked, meeting Speckle on arrival for her meeting with Alice Mulgrave and Frank Doyle.

'Can't stop now, Andy,' said Speckle, flashing past her sergeant. 'Arrange with uniform for a search of the mill on Buxton Street.'

The doors of the lift closed on Sally Speckle.

'Who'd want to be a DI, eh?' Lukeson swung around on DC Helen Rochester coming up behind him. 'The boss looks pretty stressed out.'

'A meeting with the new Assistant Chief Constable.' Lukeson took a step back. 'What's happened to you?'

'Three Ways to Lose Three Stone,' she said proudly. 'The new diet sweeping America, Sarge. Although I haven't lost three stone, just ten pounds, but I'm determined.'

DC Helen Rochester's battle with her weight was a continuous struggle. She was the unfortunate kind who put on weight by looking at food. Her problem was not helped by her fondness for canteen sticky buns. For days, sometimes even weeks, her zeal to

19

reduce her weight would give her the resolve to avoid the canteen altogether, but then her sweet-toothed alter ego would take over, and she'd head for the canteen with a grim determination that was deaf to all pleading. Then, a couple of weeks later, the next diet would kick in and would be adhered to with a missionary zeal until the next fall. Her battle with the bulge was pure Jekyll and Hyde.

'It works,' Lukeson observed. 'But lose three stone, and you'll fall between the cracks in the floorboards.'

Helen Rochester slid her hand over her new trimness. 'I spent my leave shedding.' She looked critically at the half-finished cup of coffee he had in his hand and shook her head. 'Caffeine, Andy. Not good.'

'Don't go all missionary on me.'

'What's all this about a search party?'

'Grasshopper's ears, eh. The boss thinks there's a body to be found.'

'Crikey,' the DC answered.

'Well, look at you, then.' WPC Anne Fenning was coming towards them. 'You look fantastic, Helen.'

'Thanks, Anne,' Rochester's eyes were fixed on the two sticky buns on the plate Fenning had brought from the canteen just along the hall. 'Nice buns.'

'Thanks,' Andy Lukeson said, lifting the

tail of his jacket and giving a twirl.

'Free tonight, are you, Sarge?' a passing PC commented cheekily.

'Don't like brown eyes, sweetheart,' Lukeson shot back.

When the laughter had died down, Rochester enquired, 'Is Charlie still around, Andy?'

Charlie, was DC Charlie Johnson, and why Helen had asked if he was still around was because before she had gone on leave the matter of Johnson's transfer had been on the cards. He had an on-going gripe about being overlooked in favour of Helen Rochester for the vacancy of Acting DS while Andy Lukeson had been away on a course. The gist of Charlie Johnson's complaint had been that by tradition, being the senior DC to Rochester, he had a right to be Lukeson's replacement during his absence, while Speckle had exercised her right as the DI to organize her team as she saw fit. In the broader sense, Sally Speckle's departure from tradition had not been welcomed; CS Doyle had voiced his reservations, but she had stuck to her guns, giving as the reason for her decision the need, as she had seen it, to run the police force on a business basis, making the best possible use of resources both human and technological to achieve the

21

best results, rather than as an old boys' club. Doyle's decision had been to let the dust settle before taking a decision on DC Johnson's transfer request.

'I suppose the Chief Super thinks that if he sits on Charlie's request long enough, he'll mend bridges with the DI,' Lukeson opined.

'How does the boss feel about it?'

'How would I know?'

'Oh, come on, Andy. You're her right arm.'

'If you want my opinion, I think she'd be very sorry to see the back of Charlie Johnson, as would I. His leaving would break up a pretty good team.'

Helen Rochester said, 'I wish the DI had never picked me to replace you, Andy. Her decision put me in an impossible position.'

'That's rubbish,' WPC Anne Fenning opined. 'Why should you have to feel like shit, Helen? The force, as far as promotion is concerned, has been a closed shop for too bloody long. As for female officers, the neanderthals, and there are plenty of those still around, think we should still be making tea and running errands!'

DS Andy Lukeson's smile was a wry one. 'You're not going to burn your bra in the hall are you, Fenning?'

'Typical!' Fenning pulled a face and walked off.

22

'You've put yourself in her bad books, Sarge,' Rochester said.

'I'm seldom out of someone's bad books. It's a sergeant's lot, isn't it?' he said, philosophically.

★ ★ ★

Assistant Chief Constable Alice Mulgrave sat stony-faced, her intelligent grey eyes unflinching in their perusal of DI Sally Speckle, she was an officer Mulgrave had heard nothing but good things about; obviously time-keeping was not one of her better points, however. She had been ten minutes and nine seconds late and, being an admirer and an advocate of punctuality, unpunctuality was a vice the new ACC frowned on.

At 47, Alice Mulgrave had long ago settled for a career rather than marriage, and had made her work her life. There was, on occasion, a brief liaison with a man, but nothing that had ever reached partner status, and she was realistic enough to understand that there were not many men who would come up to her expectations, which were at odds with the quick roll-in-the-hay world that she lived in. Not that she was adverse to a roll in the hay, but it had to evolve from a relationship which had in turn evolved from a period of getting to know one another, rather than the kind of lightning quick hop from pub to club to bed which was the norm of the day.

CS Frank Doyle sat alongside the ACC but, with due deference, was seated to the left of centre and, like Mulgrave, though not as much a stickler for time as she was, was not pleased and pointedly checked his watch.

'Sorry,' Speckle apologized. 'Traffic.'

The porky dropped like a stone through water.

'It can be a problem,' Mulgrave said. 'Though, arriving only twenty minutes ago, I didn't find it so, Inspector.'

Doyle was wearing what Andy Lukeson called his *bloody hell* expression, and Speckle was in no doubt that at the first opportunity Doyle would let his views be known forcefully.

'It ebbs and flows, ma'am,' Speckle said lamely, cringing under Mulgrave's steely glare.

'Then I must have been most fortunate,' Mulgrave said. 'I got all the flow and none of the ebb.' She placed a finger on the folder on the desk in front of her, the record of one Sally Speckle. 'Good work. Three murder inquiries and three convictions is admirable in your relatively short time as a DI.'

Doyle relaxed a little, but not enough yet to give Speckle some hope of avoiding a dressing-down.

'Thank you, ma'am. We were most fortunate.'

'We, Inspector?'

'The team, ma'am.'

'The *team*.' Mulgrave smiled. Doyle relaxed a little more. 'Give credit where credit is due, eh, Inspector.'

'It's only fair, ma'am.'

'Indeed it is,' Mulgrave said, her smile widening.

Doyle thought that if the Assistant Chief Constable lost a little of her starch, she could be quite a good-looking woman and, he suspected, quite playful.

'I'm a team player myself,' the ACC said. 'After all, police work is a whole lot of bits and pieces that have to make sense. Good team work makes an enormous difference.' She turned to Doyle. 'Don't you think so, Chief Superintendent?'

'Most definitely, ma'am,' he agreed. 'Team work, that's what gets the job done.'

You old fart of a hypocrite, Sally Speckle thought. Teamwork and Doyle were as alien as good and evil. He was too directorial and too dictatorial ever to be a team player. 'Bloody hogwash,' had been his often voiced opinion when team effort rather than individualism had been advocated. Obviously hitting it off with Mulgrave as Speckle seemed to be, Doyle would quickly row in and bask in the ACC's praise. Speckle saw the first glimmer of hope in avoiding the rebuke which had been inevitable only moments before.

In fact the Chief Super smiled on her benignly.

'DI Speckle is a very able officer, ma'am,' he piped up.

'Obviously so, Chief Superintendent. However . . . ' There was always an *however*. Frank Doyle's smile hovered between life and death at the possible note of criticism. 'There does seem to be some acrimony in your team, Inspector Speckle.'

Doyle scowled.

'DC Johnson's nose seems to be somewhat out of joint.'

Frank Doyle's face cried out, how the hell had the old windbag found out about that?

'Wants to be out from under your wing. Why is that, Inspector?' Mulgrave asked.

'DS Lukeson was away on a course and I needed to appoint an acting DS in his place. I chose to appoint DC Helen Rochester, ma'am.'

'Why did you see fit to go outside the

norm? Johnson had seniority on his side.'

Frank Doyle cast Speckle a look that said: Give the wrong answer to this, my girl, and your rising star will implode in the blink of an eye.

'I'm not a believer in promotion simply based on service, ma'am,' she stated flatly.

'Oh?' Alice Mulgrave intoned. 'But service equates with experience, does it not, Inspector?'

'Service has its place in the order of things,' Speckle said. 'But in my opinion there are other factors of equal importance.' Clearly, judging by the tightness of his features, Doyle had had quite enough of her opinons, and obviously wished she would keep them to herself and do as everyone else had done, namely say what the ACC wanted to hear. 'And,' Speckle continued, 'a senior officer has to take a balanced view rather than always, irrespective of circumstances, adhere slavishly to what has gone before, ma'am.'

'So, it was my opinion that DC Rochester was best suited to the task on hand. Of course, circumstances might favour DC Johnson's selection at another time, were the situation to arise.'

Frank 'Sermon' Doyle's fingers were flexing. Sally Speckle reckoned that he was imagining them round her throat. The seconds ticked by, each one the length of an hour it seemed, before Alice Mulgrave spoke.

'An admirably sensible approach, I would have thought,' she finally said. 'Wouldn't you say, Chief Superintendent?'

'Admirable,' Doyle agreed, beaming at Speckle.

'Tradition is, of course, all very fine,' Mulgrave said. 'But in these troubled times the police must use its resources to the fullest extent.'

'Absolutely, ma'am,' Doyle chipped in.

'Keep up the good work, Inspector,' Mulgrave said. 'I'll be keeping a keen eye on you.'

Sally Speckle's relief that the meeting was over, was tempered by the idea of Mulgrave keeping a keen eye on her.

'By the way, Inspector . . . '

On her way out, Sally Speckle paused mid-stride and turned. 'Ma'am?'

'Is it your wish that DC Johnson should remain as part of your team?' Alice Mulgrave enquired.

'Yes, it is, ma'am,' Speckle stated truthfully.

On reaching the hall, Speckle leaned against the wall getting her breath back. Her elation at having, in her opinion, made a reasonably good impression on the new ACC lasted all of ten seconds before what had happened earlier came flooding back to haunt her.

'How was Mulgrave?' Lukeson asked, when Speckle arrived back at her office.

'I think she'll make a good ACC, Andy,' was her honest opinion. 'Search party arranged for?'

'Two burly constables.'

'Only two?' Speckle exclaimed.

'Lucky at that.'

'When are the powers-that-be going to realize that without enough officers, the criminals are winning? How big is the mill?'

'About the size of Old Trafford. Where did this business about a body come from anyway?'

'Let's go to the canteen. My treat.'

'Your treat?' Lukeson grinned. 'Now you really have me worried.'

★ ★ ★

'Speckle around, girlie?'

Girlie.

WPC Anne Fenning's hackles were instantly at full stretch. 'DI Speckle is not available at present,' she replied frostily.

'Collected her pressie yet, has she?' asked the man on the phone.

Anne Fenning winced. Luckily for her she had not ticked him off as she had been tempted to, a man bearing gifts could mean a man in love. She had not heard that Sally Speckle had a man in her life, and it surprised her that she might have, as it would everyone else, she reckoned. Because the common perception around Loston nick was, that it was only a matter of time before her DI and DS shacked up.

'Present?'

'Obviously not.' The man was suddenly angry. 'You'd have heard about it, if she had. Tell her Fred called, girlie,' he barked.

Fenning snapped.

'Has anyone ever told you that you're an absolute tosser,' she said, causing breaths to be taken in sharply around her.

The man on the phone laughed.

'Spirited, I like that.'

WPC Anne Fenning slammed the phone down. And when her temper cooled, a little shiver ran through her, not because she had cooled down, but because she suddenly realized how menacing the man on the phone had been. She scribbled down the mobile number on caller display for passing on to Speckle.

What was Sally Speckle thinking of, going out with a creep like that?

* ★ ★

After Speckle told him about Fred, DS Andy
Lukeson sipped at his canteen coffee that
could, he reckoned, be used to fill potholes,
not wanting to ponder on what it was doing
to the lining of his stomach.

'Say something, Andy,' Speckle said.

'Well, I think you might have gone off
half-cocked. This could all be a stupid prank.
People get up to all sorts of silly things on
birthdays.'

'A prankster? Phoning from a payphone in
Loston Mental Hospital?'

'All part of the wind-up. Sinister phone call
from sinister place. Present in old mill.
Copper's mind at work. Present becomes a
body. Copper goes haring off to search the
mill. Cue, loud laughter. Copper humour is
about as twisted as it gets, Sally.'

Lukeson's chronicling of a possible birthday wind-up had Speckle doubting, but she
soon swept her doubt aside, and stated
positively, 'Fred is not a prankster, Andy.' She
told him about Fred's reference to her new
hairdo. 'And I believe he's been in my house.'

Andy Lukeson sat up.

'No signs of forced entry, but that could be
because he's a pro. There were other signs,
though.' She told him about the flattened

31

cushion and the coffee mug. 'I like everything neat and tidy. There's no way that I'd leave a shoddily washed mug or a flattened cushion.'

Andy Lukeson recalled that, even tipsy after the celebration of the successful conclusion of her first murder investigation, Sally Speckle had insisted on putting everything back in its proper place before seeing him off. A routine of fluffing cushions, washing cups and replacing them from where she had got them, even the correcting of an askew lampshade which he had bumped against. He had thought at the time that her behaviour had been a bit too fussy for his liking. He was not an untidy sod, but neither was he obsessional.

'Living alone, you get like that, Andy,' she had said, when she turned and had seen him watching her readjust the lampshade. 'The mug might have prints or DNA. And the cushion might have hairs or fibres,' she continued.

Dismissing his idea of a prankster, Lukeson said, concernedly, 'You'll need to get SOCO in.' And when Speckle was lacking in enthusiasm for the idea, 'Would you prefer to be lying with your throat cut before they went in?' Speckle shot her sergeant an alarmed look. 'My mum always said I had a big mouth.'

'A very astute woman, your mum,' Speckle flung back.

'Better safe than sorry, I say. You don't know what you're dealing with. This Fred could be just some idiot with a warped sense of humour you've tangled with, but he could also be a weirdo with a murderous fixation. And have the payphone at the hospital dusted for prints. With any luck, we might find something of interest. And let's look at their CCTV footage. A mental hospital must have a camera in every nook and cranny.'

'No CCTV. The system is being upgraded.'

'Someone in the know?'

'There's this contract cleaner called Brite. He has form for making nasty calls to women. When I phoned back, he answered the payphone. Didn't sound anything like Fred though.'

'Maybe that's because he expected you to phone back and changed his voice.'

Speckle's mobile rang.

'Anne,' she said cheerily, then her expression froze. 'Fred, did you say? His mobile number?' she asked in disbelief. 'Look, Anne, get on to the service provider. Try and get a name and address for the number. Phone me back. Oh, and, as an older generation of coppers would have said, see if he's known to the police.'

'Fred phoned and didn't bother to withold his number, Andy. Can you believe that?'

'Frankly, no,' was his blunt reply. 'It's one of four things: a massive stroke of luck; the excitement of the moment got to him; he's an idiot; or he's cocked up big time.'

'There's one other reason,' Speckle said. 'Maybe he doesn't give a toss.'

Assistant Chief Constable Mulgrave and CS Frank Doyle entered the canteen.

'Not a bad looker, the new broom,' Lukeson observed.

Sally Speckle wondered if Alice Mulgrave was Andy Lukeson's type. There was no denying her pang of jealousy.

'If I can have your attention, Sergeant,' she said stonily. 'There's also a man called Shooter, as in revolver. A musician involved in a music-therapy programme. Also in the know, I'd say. And he lives of all places on Allworth Avenue.'

'Allworth Avenue. The scene of your first triumph, that does bring back memories. Next move?'

'Let's go and talk to Brite and Shooter, Andy, before we raise a hornet's nest.'

Fenning phoned back. Speckle checked the information Anne Fenning had passed on to her: 'Alan Harper, 6 Cox Street. No form.'

'Cox Street?' Lukeson said; and then

immediately, 'A word, sir?' Lukeson was back in a moment after a brief chat with CS Doyle. 'Wrong street.'

'What're you talking about?' Speckle asked.

'It's Crescent Street, not Cox — where Mulgrave's renting a house,' he explained, to a befuddled Speckle. 'Doyle's brother-in-law's house, while he's away in America for a year.'

On their way along the hall from the canteen, Lukeson turned into the gents. 'Canteen coffee, guaranteed to create an emergency.'

'No room in the car-park so I'm parked in the street.'

A hand waved out from the closing door of the gents.

★   ★   ★

'Idiot,' Speckle chided herself on finding the driver's door of the Punto unlocked, though she was certain she had locked it. She had been in a rush for her meeting with Mulgrave and Doyle, and had also been preoccupied with Fred, not that anyone would bother stealing the Punto anyway. Getting into the car, Speckle saw a single red rose on the passenger seat. There was a handwritten card attached to it that read: *Fred. Kisses.* She got out of the car and looked both ways along the street. There were a couple of men in view, seemingly going about their business. A third man, turning into a side street looked back — Fred? She hurried after him, but on turning into the short street he had vanished. The street joined up with a very busy shopping area which would allow Fred, if Fred he was, to merge into the crowd. She did not follow. She had only got a half glimpse of the man in the distance as he sped round the corner, not enough for a positive ID, and she could hardly accost every man she came across.

Once her shock subsided, she became hopeful. She had a sample of Fred's handwriting, and that could reveal a great deal about him.

3

The man who opened the front door of 6 Cox Street was in his mid-seventies at a conservative estimate. He looked vaguely and somewhat apprehensively at his visitors.

'Mr Alan Harper?' Speckle enquired.

'Yes. I'm Alan Harper,' he said timidly.

There was no way Lukeson could see Harper as Speckle's tormentor, and by her glance his way, she was obviously of the same mind. But, of course, there was the problem of his mobile having been used. A woman, younger, possibly by ten years, appeared in the hall behind Harper in a guard dog stance.

'Who are you?' she curtly demanded to know.

'We're police officers. I'm DI Speckle and my colleague is — '

'Police?' she interjected, alarmed.

'Mrs Harper, is it?' Speckle asked.

'Miss Harper. We've paid the telly licence, you know,' she said defensively. 'I told the man who called that it was an oversight. My brother simply forgot to renew it.'

'We've come about a call that was made from Mr Harper's mobile phone,' Speckle explained.

'Alan, what call are they talking about?'

'Call?' Harper said, struggling to gather his thoughts.

'My brother's memory is not what it used to be, you know,' Miss Harper explained unnecessarily.

Harper clapped his hands together. 'Stolen!'

'Your phone was stolen, sir?' Lukeson checked.

'Of course,' Miss Harper said. 'Silly me. Alan's phone was stolen from him in the park by a vagrant.'

'When was this?' Lukeson enquired.

'Early this morning. Alan and I go to the park most mornings. It's good to get out. I warned him not to go wandering off on paths that were poorly frequented. And not to go very far. But, of course, he took no notice, did you, Alan?' she scolded him. 'He was in view one moment, and the next he was gone. By the time I found him he had been accosted by this awful man who wanted money. He'd taken a bit of a tumble, and would have probably been killed had this nice off-duty nurse not happened along to help him. When he got home, he found that his mobile phone had been stolen.'

'Can you describe the vagrant, sir?' Lukeson asked, and saw how foolish his question was on seeing Alan Harper's distant

38

look. He changed course. 'You didn't see any man who might have been responsible, Miss Harper?'

'Afraid not.'

'I think that's about it,' Speckle said. 'Thank you both for your co-operation. Before I go, I wonder' — she took her notebook from her pocket — 'if you'd mind writing your name for me, Mr Harper?'

'Write his name?' Miss Harper asked suspicously. 'I don't understand why you'd want Alan to write his name.'

'Just routine, Miss Harper,' Speckle said.

'Oh, don't fuss so, Edith,' Harper said, taking Speckle's notebook and writing in it. 'A bit of a scrawl, I'm afraid.'

'Thank you both again,' Speckle said. 'You never know, we might come across your mobile, Mr Harper.'

'Do tell them that we have the licence, won't you?' Miss Harper called after them.

'Nothing like Fred's writing, Andy,' Speckle said, glancing at Harper's signature. 'He's not a candidate anyway, is he?'

'Safely out of the picture, I reckon,' Lukeson said, getting into the Punto. 'Now we know why Fred didn't bother to withhold the number: the bastard nicked the phone.'

★ ★ ★

Having checked with the hospital, Speckle had been told that Larry Brite had gone home sick; the time of his departure, within minutes of having spoken to her, was interesting. The woman who opened the door of the house on the Clewbridge Estate (a council warren of malcontent) glanced with unerring recognition at the police and enquired, 'What do you lot want, then?' and added belligerently, 'My Larry ain't done nothin'.'

'Then he has nothing to worry about,' Lukeson said stiffly.

'Pull the other!'

'We'd like to talk to your husband, Mrs Brite,' Speckle said.

'Well, you can't. He's in bed. Tummy. Larry's got an ulcer, ya know. Not that you lot would care, would ya?'

'Mind if we come in. It won't take a moment.' Mrs Brite moved to block Andy Lukeson from entering. Speckle wondered what he was up to. He'd know that he could not barge his way in uninvited, not without a search warrant. 'He's not here at all, is he?' Lukeson guessed, shrewdly.

'Look,' Mrs Brite said desperately, 'if the company Larry works for found out, he'd get the push.'

'Where is he?' Speckle enquired.

40

'He's doin' a bit of paintin' on the side. It ain't easy, ya know. Five kids.'

Sally Speckle thought, well, at least it's a more innocent reason for Brite's quick departure from the hospital.

'You won't tell 'em, will ya?' Mrs Brite pleaded. 'The contractors, I mean.'

'The relationship between your husband and his employer is none of our concern, Mrs Brite,' Speckle said. 'But we do need to talk to him.'

'He's round at Mr Moser's place.'

'And where would that be?'

'The Grove. Them posh houses near the rugby club. Number eleven.'

'Thank you.'

Speckle looked at the muddy patch that served as the Brite garden — not a weed, let alone a rose flourished on it.

On the way to the Punto, Lukeson said, 'She'll be on the blower to him.'

'No way to stop her, Andy, without sitting on her. And we don't want complaints of police harrassment, do we.'

'Of course not. That would upset our new Assistant Chief Constable.'

'Don't be so bloody cynical.' Speckle paused. 'Or are you implying that I'm putting career before crime?'

'No.'

'I'm not sure I believe you, Sergeant.'

'What can I say . . . ma'am?' There was a brooding standoff, until Lukeson said, 'Of course, I don't believe you're putting career before crime. So can we get on with it? Or are we going to stand around in this godawful place staring each other down?'

'Haven't you got any respect for senior officers?'

'Not much. More for you than most.'

Speckle smiled.

'Lucky me then. We'll be passing Allworth Avenue on the way to the Grove. It might be an idea to pop in on Shooter, rather than back tracking.'

'You're the boss,' Lukeson said. 'Your wish is my command.'

Her smile broadened. 'Sometimes you can be the arsehole of all arseholes, Andy.'

★   ★   ★

'Nice red roses,' Lukeson said, pointing to a bed of roses in Rupert Shooter's unblemished garden.

Speckle pressed the doorbell. Shooter responded instantly, not bothering to hide his annoyance at their presence.

'Inspector Speckle,' he greeted Sally, ironically. 'I do hope that this visit will not be

42

as devastating as your previous one. Knocked the property prices for six, that did. Had to withdraw my house from sale. Nothing much has changed. Still can't sell it for what it would have been worth,' he said peevishly.

Shooter was referring to Allworth Avenue's role in Speckle's first murder inquiry, referred to in the press as the 'Pick Up' case. Clearly, Shooter was seeing her as the reason for his house sale woes.

'And as always, accompanied by the faithful hound dog DS Lukeson,' Shooter intoned.

'You have a good memory, Mr Shooter,' Lukeson said.

'It's easy to recall the unforgettable, Sergeant,' Shooter said.

It was not a compliment.

'May we come in?' Speckle asked.

Shooter stepped aside. 'First room on the right.' The first room on the right turned out to be a small cluttered office. 'Well?' Shooter asked narkily. 'I do hope this will be brief, I'm rather busy.' As there was only one chair, which Shooter quickly took possession of standing was compulsory.

Shooter's voice was somewhat deeper in tone than Fred's, Speckle noted. But then perhaps if heard over the phone . . . electronic transmission can change a voice.

'You were at Loston Mental Hospital this morning at around 9.30,' Speckle stated. 'Did you see a man using the payphone in reception?'

'Yes.'

'Did you recognize this man?'

'No'

'Can you describe him, then?'

'He was a man using the payphone, Inspector. He had his back turned to me. An impression is the best I can do.'

'And that impression was?'

'Oh . . . muscular, going to seed.'

'Is that it?' Lukeson questioned.

'He was a patient.'

'How can you be sure of that, Mr Shooter?' Speckle asked.

'Dressing-gown. On his way to hydro-therapy. Dr Ekstein's programme,' he said, in as near a scoff as didn't matter. The way he said, '*American, you know*,' left no doubt as to his low opinion of Americans. His statement, 'Of what possible use splashing about in water can be, I can't imagine,' left no doubt that his opinion of Americans also applied to their treatments.

Perhaps to those taking part, every bit as useful as music-therapy, Speckle might have opined another time.

'How can you be sure that this patient was

44

on his way to hydrotherapy?' Lukeson questioned.

'He was wearing a green dressing-gown. Simple, but quite ingenious, you know. Patients in different programmes and treatments wear different colour dressing-gowns,' Shooter explained. 'That way staff can tell at a glance who's who and what's what, and where everyone should be. Mr Thomas's idea, and an admirable one I must say. Music-therapy is a rather fetching sky blue.'

'Did *you* use the phone, Mr Shooter?' Speckle questioned.

'Me, use a public phone.' His astonishment was genuine. 'Heaven forbid.'

'Would you mind giving me a sample of your handwriting?'

'I'd mind very much, Inspector. Unless you can give me a good, a very good reason, why I should.'

'We won't take up any more of your time,' Speckle said.

'You'll see yourself out,' Shooter said, turning away.

'Can't have been a patient,' Lukeson said on leaving. 'A patient could not be out and about commiting murder.'

'The dressing-gown could have been worn to hide a uniform, maybe,' Speckle suggested. 'A logo or a company name on contract personnel, perhaps?'

'Shooter didn't like the idea of giving a hand-writing sample, did he?' Lukeson said. 'Maybe he knew that you had a sample to compare it with.' He paused. 'One of those roses might prove to be interesting, if the lab could get hold of one. Soil it was grown in. Pesticides and nutrients used. Local environmental factors. Maybe, with luck, even a speck of blood for DNA after the prick of a thorn, if we should need it.'

'Andy!' Speckle chided, as Lukeson nipped across the lawn and plucked a rose. 'That, at best, could be vandalism. And at worst, theft.'

'We have a rose to match. And wouldn't it be very interesting if Shooter were to get all hot under the collar about a humble copper nicking a rose from his garden.'

'How could he? He'll hardly have counted them and check when you've gone.'

'Don't look now. Upstairs. Top right-hand corner window. The corner of the curtain has just dropped into place when I glanced up. You know, maybe all this is because you cocked up the sale of his house.'

'Don't be daft, Andy. People don't commit murder because they can't sell their houses.'

'Obviously Shooter blames you for his woes, boss. Who knows what problems you might have caused him? Imagine if it brought

46

about his financial ruin. Or great financial distress.'

'If Shooter did feel aggrieved, why would he wait until now?'

'Maybe over time, because he couldn't flog his house, his financial problems worsened and his anger with you intensified.'

'A bit fanciful, Andy.'

'What's fanciful to you or me, might not be to Shooter.'

'So why didn't he simply kill *me*?'

Lukeson shrugged. 'Good question, if you're sane. But logic and madness are not bedfellows, Sally. Maybe he prefers to torment you. Or ruin you. If you can't catch Fred it'd be a kind of, you ruined me, so I'll ruin you.'

★ ★ ★

'Ain't no one home,' Larry Brite said, the instant he opened the front door of 11 The Grove, and went to close it again.

Lukeson put his hand on the door to stop it closing. 'I'm sure your employers would be pleased to know about your swift and miraculous recovery, Brite.'

'DI Sally Speckle. We spoke on the phone this morning, Mr Brite.'

'Oh, yeah. You wanted to know where you

47

was phonin', right?'

'I'll come straight to the point, Brite,' Speckle said. 'Did you phone me, before I phoned you back?'

'Why would I do that? You're a perfect stranger.'

'So were those other women you phoned.'

For a moment, Brite seemed cornered, then obviously a way out opened up. 'What time did you get this phone call, eh?'

'About nine thirty,' Speckle said.

'There you are, then! About that time I was in Mr Thomas's office chasin' a mouse what ran' cross his desk.' He chuckled. 'Nearly wet himself. Now, can I get back to painting?'

'Mind if I ask you for a sample of your handwriting, Brite?'

Brite, seemingly unconcerned by Speckle's request, joked, 'I knew someday I'd be famous.'

'Or infamous,' Lukeson chipped in.

Brite handed back Speckle her notebook and pen. 'Same thing, ain't it, mate?'

'Don't get a dizzy spell and fall off your ladder, will you, Mr Brite?' Lukeson said sarcastically.

The front door of 11 The Grove slammed in Speckle and Lukeson's faces. Walking to the Punto, Lukeson observed, 'Nice garden, but not a rose to be seen.'

48

'I reckon that rules Brite out,' Speckle said. 'He's too well versed in police ways for him to think that we wouldn't check his alibi. And he had no objection to giving a sample of his handwriting.'

She studied his signature.

'Could be some similarity to Fred's, but not a match, I reckon,' was her opinion. 'Then, of course, if he knew what we were after, Brite could have altered his handwriting.'

'Would Brite waste his time trying?' Lukeson wondered. 'He has form, so we'll have his proper signature on file for comparison. And no matter how you try, you can't completely change your handwriting. There's always some quirk that shows through.'

'Better go through the motions.' Speckle punched out the number of Loston Mental Hospital on her mobile and requested to speak with Thomas, who confirmed what Brite had told them. 'That's Brite out of the frame.' Getting into the Punto she said, 'Let's search that old mill, Andy.'

4

On entering the abandoned former textile mill on Buxton Street, the first thing that struck them was its smell — a gut-wrenching cocktail of fetid air.

'Something's dead in here!' exclaimed PC Alan Dunnett, the younger of the uniformed duo assisting Speckle and Lukeson in the search of the mill.

'Foul death, indeed, me thinks,' said PC Smith, authoritively and bravely sniffing the air. Smith was into amateur dramatics and, at 42, still held out the hope that one day he'd be *spotted*.

Andy Lukeson's sigh was long and weary. 'A needle in a haystack, isn't it.' He looked about at the debris-strewn mill. 'We'd need a small army to search this place effectively.'

'I don't think so, Andy,' Speckle said. 'If this nutter Fred's gift is a dead body, he'll want to present it to me. So if it's here, it will be on display, I reckon.' She turned to the PCs. 'OK, then, start shining those nice police issue torches you've brought along. You take the left,' she instructed Dunnett. 'You,

50

the right, PC Smith. We'll take the centre ground, Andy.'

★ ★ ★

An hour later, dusty and barely breathing, Speckle led the search party out of the mill having found nothing.

'Maybe we should look for more man-power,' Lukeson proposed. 'It's a warren in there. Blink and you'd miss something.'

'Are you sure there's no other old mill, Andy?'

'This is the only one.'

'There's the pub,' PC Dunnett said.

'I doubt if we'd find a body in a pub,' Speckle said.

Dunnett laughed. 'You'd be liable to find all sorts in there, in its day, ma'am. Used to be a haunt of mine when I was younger.' Speckle wondered how much younger, seeing that Dunnett could not be older than his late twenties. 'Archie Tattan, the owner, used to grandiosely call it a roadhouse. Flush the loo and come away with it on your shoes.'

'Charming,' Smith intoned, at a pitch to reach the balcony.

'Where is this place, Dunnett?' Speckle asked.

'Closer to Brigham than Loston, ma'am,

but it's on Loston's patch. I know, because it was rozzers from Loston who'd raid the place. Shut its doors about a year ago. It's off the beaten track, on a side road, you see. Suppose that's what did for it in the end and, of course, the odd case of food poisoning and the flat beer didn't help.'

'Lead the way, Constable,' Speckle said.

★   ★   ★

The country road leading to the former Old Mill pub, aka the roadhouse, was just about wide enough for a single vehicle. Bordered by deep dykes on either side, a slight error of judgement could see a car ditched. The low-hanging trees, whose branches in some parts brushed the roof of the car, did not help, serving only to darken the road on what was already a dark day. It had begun to drizzle, and a rolling fog reduced visibility, adding to the road's treachery. As Dunnett had said, the access road to it had probably been the reason for the pub's demise. It would not have been a hostelry to leave with one too many, Speckle thought.

They came round a sharp bend, one of a series in a little over a mile of road, and there it was — the Old Mill. For a building that had only closed a year ago, it was surprisingly dilapidated; vandals had made it look more like twenty. The place looked as though a good winter storm would bring the entire structure crashing down. The entrance doors had been forced open, and if the inside of the Old Mill matched the outside, better that the entire building be pulled down rather than any attempt be made to restore it. It had the look and feel of a place that would rot away, until one day it would simply blow away on the wind.

Leading the way inside, PC Dunnett came up short, spun around and vomited. Smith, a step behind, also came up short but, more hardened to the surprises and horrors of police work was more shockproof.

'Not a pretty sight, ma'am,' Smith warned, when Speckle forged ahead.

Her present, the blood-soaked body of a woman, was lying on the bar counter. A red rose lay on the blood-drenched white dressing-gown she wore. The greeting card looped round the big toe of her right foot was identical to the one Speckle had found in her car. Its message was the same: *Fred. Kisses.*

The woman had no face.

Speckle was not sure whether the blood-soaked name of Claire on the pocket of the dressing-gown was the dressing-gown's brand name, or the victim's monogram.

'Come on, then,' Fred coaxed the duck waddling up to where he sat feeding crumbs to the pigeons. He liked coming to the park. There were a lot of old fogeys gadding about, pretending they were fitter than they really were, and trying to look younger, stupidly chasing their youth that had been lost a long time ago. He hated old people. They smelled. Nothing more pathetic than to see them feigning forced cheeriness over the joint pains that made them grimace. And he found their false optimism, when any breath could be their last, irritating.

However, in the overall balance, the park was a haven from the annoying world beyond its gates, and Fred could think there, make plans there.

A couple of months ago a man had been murdered on the bench he was now sitting on.[1] Throat slashed from ear to ear. He had been in the park that day, and it had excited him to have been so close to violent death. He could smell the old man's blood. There had been a lot of it. He had liked its smell, and it had been with him ever since. All he had to do was sniff and there it was, the

---

[1] See *Remains Found*

warm, sweet scent of fresh blood. Claire Shaw's blood had smelled differently, more pungent than the old man's blood had been. It had smelled . . . tainted. He supposed he knew the reason for that.

'Don't be a wimp,' Fred rebuked the duck, who was scared off by an aggressive pigeon. Coaxed, the duck waddled forward bravely. 'That's it. Take no shit.' But at the last second, faced with a squawking crow, the duck fled. 'Bloody wimp!' he growled. He took a small green glass bottle from his pocket containing brandy. It was the kind one might have found in a hospital lab or a pharmacy in times past, when presciptions did not come ready made and had to be dispensed. Often such a bottle would have contained poison. He never used clear glass for spirits since he had received a look of disapproval from an old fogey. The brandy kept out the chill and, fortified, he got up and, scattering the pigeons and crows, he dropped some crumbs. Encouraged, the duck came to feed on the bread. Fred gave the duck time to get used to his presence. 'There's a good fellow,' he crooned, offering some more crumbs. He glanced about and, seeing no one nearby, poured brandy over the duck's back. He lit a match and casually tossed it on to the bird. The alcohol immediately ignited. He enjoyed watching the duck attempting to shake off the flames, screeching pitifully as it burned. He turned and walked away, toying with the idea of burning his next victim.

On seeing the woman approaching, walking a prim little poodle (he hated small poofy dogs) Fred wiped the smile from his face.

She'd think he was crazy, laughing to himself.

★ ★ ★

No one moved for a long time, cruelly mesmerized as they were by the gruesome sight. Andy Lukeson was the first to speak. 'Jesus, mercy.' He had not sworn. He had prayed. He crossed himself.

5

'Vile,' said Alec Balson, the police surgeon. 'There's a lot of madness in this murder, I think. Dead about twelve hours, give or take either side, which would put her murder at about two a.m.' He looked closer. 'Without a face to help us identify her' — Speckle and Lukeson leaned closer to see the tattoo of a football with crossed daggers on the top of the woman's arm to which Balson was pointing — 'visual identification will be a non-starter. Dental records, fingerprints and DNA.' He looked inside her mouth. 'Looks like a recent filling in a back wisdom tooth, right side. Might mean she attended a Loston dentist.'

Balson leaned back.

'The bastard really had a go, didn't he?'

'Perhaps he wanted to delay recognition,' Lukeson said. 'Maybe quick identification would point a finger directly at her killer. He might have needed time to reach some place like South America.'

'I'd opt for pure insanity,' Balson opined. 'The stomach of a sane man would be hard put to take this slaughter.'

'Murder weapon, Alec?' Speckle asked.

Balson examined the woman's shattered face.

'Don't hold me to this,' he said, 'but, see these deep curved ridges in the remaining flesh, they suggest something round and weighty; a heavy poker, perhaps. The frenzy of the attack might indicate a sexual motive, such as pleasure from inflicting pain. However, it could also be that his rage stems from possible impotency. Maybe the killer just can't get his jollies in the normal way, and destroys the object of his desire because he can't fulfil that desire, and vents his rage on the woman who has highlighted his shortcomings.'

Alec Balson chuckled throatily.

'Will you just listen to a humble GP spouting Freudian theories? Of course, you know that it all began because his mother always gave him soggy cornflakes for breakfast.'

'You're not a disciple of psychoanalysis, I take it,' Lukeson said.

'It has it's values,' Balson said. 'But . . . ' He looked at the battered woman. 'Often nowadays fancy excuses are found for what is simply pure evil.'

Balson stood up stiffly.

'I must remember to take my daily dose of

cod liver oil. There'll be no mistaking the place where she was murdered. It would have been awash with blood. Prelim report, as always, as soon as poss.'

'Why here?' Speckle said, when Balson left. 'Why murder her and bring her here, Andy?'

'It was a pub. Past associations. Maybe Fred worked here, or was a customer. Did the dead woman work here? Or, again, was she the customer and her killer the employee? Take your pick. First of all, I think we should find the owner of this place.'

'Finding Archie Tattan won't be easy,' said PC Dunnett. 'He took off when he crossed a nastier bastard than himself. Rotten bugger, was Archie Tattan. Headed for trouble since he popped out of his mother's womb.'

'If you were a regular here — '

'I wouldn't say regular, ma'am,' Dunnett corrected.

Speckle ignored the correction.

' — you must have known the staff who worked here?'

'There weren't many full-time staff. Tattan used casuals to fill in, at weekends and bank holidays. He and his wife, Lindy, Tattan's equal in nastiness, did most of what needed doing.'

'Let's start with the full-timers,' Lukeson said.

'There was Judy Mayhew, the barmaid. And there was Jack Ansome, a general handyman and dogsbody who pulled pints when needed. Ansome was a moody sod. Didn't have much to say for himself. I used to joke that if he wanted to, he'd make a very good cat burglar. Could move about the place like a ghost. One second he was nowhere to be seen, and the next he was right at your elbow.'

'That silent, was he?' Speckle said thoughtfully, images of Fred creeping about her house springing to mind.

'Used to give Betty, my girlfriend at the time, the creeps. She said she caught him looking at her a couple of times like she was a tasty morsel.'

'A tasty morsel?'

'Yes, Sarge. Meaning that she thought he fancied her, in a weird sort of way, she said, but Betty Branfield was an artist. Sometimes her imagination would run away with her.'

'Cat burglar,' Speckle murmured. 'Do you know if Ansome was good with locks? Opening them, I mean without leaving a trace?'

'Never heard him mention it, but he did say that he had had to do everything for himself on the mission fields, and that's how he was so handy. You can't ring up an electrician or a plumber in the bush, Ansome would say.'

'Ansome was a former priest?'

'Yes, ma'am.'

'RC? or C of E?'

'RC,' Dunnett confirmed.

'You're sure?'

'Oh, yes. One night a bloke who'd had one too many saw the Pope on telly and said something nasty about him. Next thing, Jack Ansome had him by the throat.'

'Sounds like he was a devout Catholic, doesn't it?' Lukeson said.

'A bit more than devout I'd say, Sarge,' Dunnett said. 'Could go on a bit if anyone spoke or acted out of turn. Tattan had to pull his leash now and then. 'There's no bloody pulpit here Ansome', Tattan would say.'

'A bit of a zealot, then?'

'Yeah, Sarge. I reckon that would be Jack Ansome all right.'

DI Sally Speckle raised an eyebrow. 'So if Ansome was such an ardent RC, why was he a *former* priest and not a serving minister? Never said why he left the priesthood, did he?'

'No.'

'Or why the church might have left him?' Lukeson said.

'No, Sarge. That I know of, no one ever asked.'

'Why was that?' Lukeson enquired.

'Like I said, Ansome was a moody bugger. He had a short fuse and was best left to himself — that was the general view.' Dunnett looked around him. 'A funny old place to have ended up, isn't it? But then, what is a bloke qualified to do after being a priest? Not much call for God talk in any other job, is there?'

'Did Ansome say where he was on mission?'

'Talked about the bush. So I took it to be Africa, ma'am.'

'The Roman church is divided between secular and order clergy. Missionaries. Never mentioned an order, did he?'

'Don't think so,' Dunnett said. 'But he could have. I wouldn't know one RC order from the next, ma'am.'

'And Judy Mayhew?' Lukeson enquired.

'Oh, Judy was what kept this place going for as long as it did, Sarge. Great crack, was Judy. Always ready to join in whatever banter was going on. Her nickname was *Knockers*.' Without realizing the provocative nature of his gesture in Speckle's presence, Dunnett cupped his hands like a goalkeeper clutching an oversized football ready to kick out. A flick of Andy Lukeson's eyes alerted Dunnett to his gaffe, and the PC's hands became hands he did not know what to do with.

'A big girl, indeed, Constable,' Sally Speckle said, mischievously.

Alan Dunnett's feet shifted, searching for the hole in the floor into which he would gladly fall.

'Good fun, you say?' Lukeson said. 'Meaning what exactly?'

'Ah . . . ' Dunnett floundered, reluctant to be explicit in Speckle's presence. One gaffe was enough to be going on with.

'Was Judy Mayhew a slag?' Speckle asked bluntly.

Relieved that the DI had chosen not to mince her words, Dunnett replied, 'Well, there was talk, ma'am.'

'Talk?'

'I heard stories about her being . . . *willing.*'

'How did Ansome react to her?' Lukeson asked.

'Well, they weren't exactly friends, Sarge.'

'Would it be fair to say that Jack Ansome didn't approve of Judy Mayhew's extra-curricular activities?'

'Nicely put, Andy,' Speckle said, tongue-in-cheek.

'I reckon so,' Dunnett said.

'Did Ansome take issue with her?'

'No, Sarge. Not in a bust-up way. Judy

would go into a huddle with some bloke near closing time. Ansome would glare at her, and she'd glare back.'

'It never went further than that?'

'Once, outside, I saw Ansome put legs under a bloke. Judy clattered him, and he might have thumped her if I hadn't been around.'

'You mentioned casuals at weekends and busy periods?'

'They came and went, ma'am. But there was this younger bloke who was pretty regular called Benny Frederics. Collected the glasses and cleaned the tables. Not that most of the tables were well past just a wipe of a damp cloth.'

'What sort was he?'

'He was OK, ma'am.'

'How did he get on with Ansome?'

'Fine at the start. As I understood, Ansome actually got Frederics the job. Peas in a pod at first, but they had a falling out. Frederics made no secret of the fact that he wouldn't mind a roll in the hay with Judy Mayhew, and that rightly got up Ansome's nose. One night he gave Frederics a telling off about sins of the flesh. Frederics told him to get stuffed, and after that it was all downhill.'

'Did Ansome fancy Mayhew himself? Was the bust up between him and Frederics down to jealousy, perhaps?'

'Don't reckon so. Ansome saw himself as Judy's protector from sin. Ansome needn't have bothered. Judy liked the good things in life. Benny Frederics hadn't two pennies to rub together. But she might have obliged Frederics to get up Ansome's nose. Probably the kind of thing Judy would have enjoyed doing.'

Dunnett frowned.

'Like Betty Branfield, Frederics used to say that he wouldn't turn his back on Ansome. Gave him the shivers, he said. Frederics was RC in his beliefs, the little he had, but C of E in his church attendance.'

'And Ansome's reaction?'

'He'd give Frederics a right old bollic — dressing down, ma'am,' Dunnett quickly amended. 'Sometimes when Frederics would get pissed, he'd have a go at Ansome.'

'In what way?'

'He'd stand inside the bar and hold up a glass of beer as a chalice and mock the consecration of the Host. Ansome would be fit to be tied, and he wasn't the only one. No one saw much call for that kind of carry on. One night, after his sacriligious antics, Frederics got a right hammering. Put him in hospital. The talk was that Ansome had taken it on himself to teach Frederics a lesson. He was found in an alley near his flat.'

'Where was that?'

'Brigham, Sarge.'

'Can you recall the address?'

Dunnett shook his head.

'All I know is that it was near an old folks' club. Benny Frederics hated old people, old fogeys as he called them. Said they smelled. Always moaned about living near an old farts' club, as he called it.'

Andy Lukeson moved aside to make a phone call on his mobile to Brigham police.

'Do you know the present whereabouts of any of these people?' Speckle enquired of PC Alan Dunnett.

'Tattan vanished, God knows where. Ansome and Benny Frederics might have fallen off the planet. Judy Mayhew gave up her part-time status. Plies her trade on Adeline Street in Loston.'

'She'll be easy to find, then,' Speckle said. 'And, with a modicum of luck, the electoral roll will throw up Frederics and Ansome.'

'I don't reckon that Ansome and Frederics would be the voter type, ma'am,' Dunnett said. 'There could be a route to Frederics through welfare though,' he suggested. 'Rehab, too. He had the beginnings of needle tracks on his arms.'

'And Tattan's wife, Lindy?'

He pointed to the ceiling first and then the floor. 'Fell off a railway platform blind drunk shortly after the Old Mill put up the shutters.'

'You've been very helpful, Constable,' Speckle said.

'Brigham's got three old folks' clubs,' Andy Lukeson reported. 'One just a stone's throw from the nick, with an alley running alongside. DS Bob Long remembers the Frederics assault. Says that Frederics didn't want anything done about it. At the time he was living at 13 Archer Street — unlucky thirteen. Doesn't know if he's still there.'

Alec Balson popped his head in the door.

'Forgot. Bad news, I'm afraid,' he told Speckle. 'Sid Fields is away in Eygpt. Hols. Alison Crewe is standing in.' Speckle groaned. 'She's a very capable pathologist. Meticulous. Nothing wrong with that. Clear and concise work can be quite a virtue when a case comes to court. Judges and juries like conciseness.'

'The problem is, with suspects going further into the mists of time with every passing hour, coppers can't afford to hang about,' Speckle said.

'Want me to have a word?' Balson offered. 'No.'

Balson shrugged. 'Your call. Good luck.'

A time before, when Fields had torn ankle

ligaments while rock climbing, Crewe had also been his replacement, and right from the second she and Speckle had met it was petrol to flame. A suspicious death that had turned out to be a suicide. And matters had quickly gone downhill when Speckle had taken issue with Alison Crewe's reluctance to offer an opinion. 'Pathology is a science, not a parlour game,' had been Crewe's waspish riposte when Speckle suggested that an opinion might help to give the investigation direction. A subsequent inquiry, initiated by Speckle's complaint, had come down on her side which, she was certain, would not lead to any more harmonious relations with Crewe this time out.

Andy Lukeson said, 'Balson could have smoothed your path with Crewe.'

'Is that a criticism, Andy?' Speckle enquired, tetchily.

'No. Just an opinion. Which I should have obviously kept to myself.'

Speckle took the conversation back to police business.

'About Alec Balson's idea that the killer could be acting out of rage against women, Ansome's a former priest. Maybe he got into a relationship that caused him to have a crisis of faith. Hates himself for falling by the wayside. Saw the woman as evil, and now he

68

see's all women as evil? And in his twisted way, thinks they have to be punished. Not all that unusual. Men never blame themselves, do they?'

'It's a theory,' Lukeson said, non-committally.

'Oh, don't spoil me with too much praise, please,' Speckle shot back.

'Ansome's gripe could simply be with the church he served,' Lukeson said. 'Based on Dunnett's profile of Ansome, he comes across as the old-fashioned type of clergyman, the sin and retribution kind, a man still on a mission, the kind of man who might question and challenge church authority, for what he might see as a softly softly approach. A loose cannon. And no one, including the Catholic church, likes loose cannons about the place going off half-cocked, usually at the most inopportune time. And that could be the reason for the Roman church parting company with him, rather than the other way round. Hell fire and brimstone are right out of fashion. Now it's all love and forgiveness, isn't it. None of this pointing the righteous finger anymore, even at what in times past would have been seen as evil. When did you last hear a sermon about burning in hell?'

Not all that long ago, Speckle thought. Her mind went back to when her brother was dying of AIDS, and a hospital chaplain had more or less told him that he was paying the price for his wayward ways. He was only one man, with one opinion, but she had reacted by damning all priests. Someday, when the hurt eased, she would probably return to the fold. But right now, embittered as she was, she could see no point.

'OK,' Speckle said. 'Taking your gripe theory, Andy, maybe Ansome, the zealot, went a step too far to madness. And if Ansome thought that the church had gone soft on sinners, he might very well have taken their chastisement on himself. It will be interesting to find out if the dead woman was, as Ansome might see her, a loose woman. It could be the motive for her murder.'

'We've got to start somewhere,' Lukeson said. 'Why not with the theory that Ansome, a righteous zealot, has begun running amok? Of course, it could be a lot of hot air, if the motive for murder lies in your past, guv.'

'Some bloody birthday, eh, Andy!' DI Sally Speckle groaned.

6

Fred strolled through the crowds at the market on Grey's Quay. He liked the market; he liked its hustle and bustle, its humour and haggling. At the market he could move through the crowd unnoticed, be anonymous, the way he liked it. He did not mind crowds, in fact, the bigger the crowd the more comfortable he felt, the more anonymous he became. He was used to crowds. It was people, individuals, who annoyed him. They never seemed to understand that he liked to think and not to chatter. And, of course, he was only too aware from past experience that there was always the danger of saying too much, revealing too much of oneself and one's inner thoughts.

Therein, lay the path to trouble.

Claire Shaw had been one of the few people with whom he had struck up a friendship. There was a time when he thought that they might . . . but then she started an affair, and he realized Claire Shaw's true nature: She was prepared to sell herself for the good things in life, not that she'd have seen it that way, but that's what it really was

71

— prostitution. The glitzier kind, but still prostitution. That had made him as mad as hell. Claire Shaw, whom he had really thought was a good person was like everyone else, grasping and greedy and prepared to do anything if the price was right.

He was neither a compulsive nor an impulsive buyer and always took his time over a purchase, wandering through the stalls to check out what else was on offer, comparing goods and prices. Once, and only once, had he been hoodwinked. And that was with a mantel clock which struck the hour on every quarter. At first it had annoyed him. However, before he had got back to the market to tell the trader where he could stick the clock he had got used to it, and had begun to see the clock's oddness as its uniqueness.

Wandering aimlessly and not looking where he was going, Fred bumped against a woman carrying a porcelain flower pot which fell from her grasp.

'Blind, are you?' she screamed at him, brushing aside his apology.

'It was an accident,' he said, taking in the auburn beauty from head to toe in a single appraisal.

'Clumsy sod!'

Fred hated the attention the woman's

tirade was focusing on him, and had he the courage he would have throttled her then and there.

'Please, let me replace it or pay for it.'

'Oh, piss off.' She strode off, flinging back, 'A guide dog might be an idea.'

It took a moment for the crowd to refocus their attention, but it was a moment that burned into his brain, starting in its dark recesses the bubbling hatred that would grow and grow until it could not be contained any longer. Then it would burst forth, like the water from behind a breached hydro-dam.

He went to the nearest stall, having no interest at all in the ornaments the woman was flogging, intent only on fiddling about to cover his real intention. He picked up the first ornament to hand and held it up to the light by way of examining it, but it was a ruse to look after the auburn-haired woman as she strutted away.

'It's a nice piece, ain't it?' said the stall-holder.

'Not bad,' Fred agreed.

'Buyin', are ya?'

Fred shook his head.

'Then put it back,' the woman said sourly. 'Twit,' she added, as he walked away after the woman.

He panicked and quickened his pace when

the crowd suddenly grew and the woman vanished, but he was forced to fall back when the crowd thinned again and he was closer to the woman than he wanted to be. He hoped she would not turn around until he merged into the crowd again.

⋆ ⋆ ⋆

'Thought it was serious when I saw you lot in droves round here. I said to meself, Charlie, somethin's rotten on your doorstep, me old son.' He looked down on the dead woman. 'Right, weren't I?'

DI Sally Speckle swung round on hearing the man's voice behind her. He was near to where they were preparing the murdered woman for removal. 'And you are?' she questioned tersely.

'Tingster's the name. Charlie Tingster.'

'This is a crime scene, Mr Tingster. How did you get in here?' Speckle's gaze flashed accusingly to the WPC standing guard at the entrance to the Old Mill; a gaze that promised at the very least, a stiff verbal reprimand.

'Don't blame her,' Tingster said, reading Speckle's intention. 'Came in the side door, didn't I.'

'Side door?' Speckle's eyes sought out the

door Tingster spoke of.

He pointed. 'Behind that load of old junk over there. It ain't no proper door. The door's part of the wall. It was a bolthole when you lot come round to give Archie grief. That would be Archie Tattan. He owned this dump. Asked me to keep an eye on the old place until he reopened.' He looked around at the crumbling structure. 'He'd want to be quick, wouldn't he? If someone farts the place is likely to cave in. Fella by the name of Jack Ansome, who used to work here, grandly called it the Elizabethan door,' Tingster elaborated. 'Like them priest holes the Cathos had during the Reformation. A right nutter, was Ansome. Rant and rave about sinners with the best of 'em. Used to be a priest. And so uptight was our Jack, that in essence he still was. Handed me a right bollickin' one night when I tried to get off with the barmaid. Ansome told me that I'd burn for all time in hell for lustin' after Judy.'

He laughed.

'I told him that if ev'ry bloke who'd poked Judy ended up in Hell, there'd be no room left for the bleedin' fire.'

Both Speckle and Lukeson reckoned that they had on their hands, that bane of a copper's life, a person who liked the sound of their own voice best of all.

'Bet she'd have hated ending up here,' he said, nodding in the direction of the dead woman being borne away.

'Wait up,' Speckle ordered the bearers. 'Are you saying that the dead woman is Judy Mayhew, Mr Tingster?'

'Judy? Naw. It'll be Claire Shaw.'

'Claire Shaw?'

'Yeah.'

'How can you be sure?'

'It's that,' Tingster pointed to the tattoo on the woman's arm. A football with crossed daggers. 'Only saw one like that before, and that was on Claire Shaw. Same height. Same colour roof thatch too beneath all that blood.'

'Ms Shaw, was it?' Speckle enquired.

'Reckon so. Keepin' it for Mr Right, she said.' There was a sudden note of bitterness in Tingster's voice. 'Mr Right bein' some bloke with a wad to match the Bank of England reserves.'

'Did Ms Shaw frequent the Old Mill?'

'Now and then. Much too hoity-toity to mix with the lot who came here though.' He laughed meanly. 'Too posh when she was alive, and now here she is. Funny old world, ain't it?'

'You seem to be taking Ms Shaw's death in your stride, Mr Tingster,' said DS Andy Lukeson.

'I ain't goin' to break down and cry, mate.' He shook his head, his smile wry. 'Frank ain't never goin' to get in her knickers now.'

'Frank?' Lukeson prompted.

'Mellor. Frank Mellor. Claire Shaw worked at his place. Mellors Service Station, just as you turn off the Brigham road to come here.' Lukeson recalled passing the station and convenience shop. 'Don't know where she got her airs and graces from,' he said bitterly. 'She was just a checkout op. Topped, was she? A stupid question, with her lookin' like that.'

He chuckled irreverently.

'Unless she cut herself shavin'.'

It was at times like this that Speckle saw how much of a failure contraception had been.

'How well did you know Ms Shaw?' she asked, not bothering to keep her opinion of Tingster out of her voice.

'Didn't know her all that well. When I filled up at Mellors, I'd pass the time of day with her.' He nudged Andy Lukeson. 'First time, my eyes popped, I can tell ya, skimpy top and bum-hugging jeans. She were a right stopper.'

'Mellor had a job keepin' the pumps goin', so brisk was the demand. 'Best thing I ever did, takin' Claire on', he told me. 'Make me a bloody millionaire in no time at all, Charlie'. That's what he said.'

'Do you know if Mellor succeeded in, as you so quaintly put it, getting into her knickers?' Lukeson enquired.

Tingster shook his head.

'Nearly busted his water pump tryin'. But I don't reckon he did. Claire Shaw had bigger fish in mind than Frankie boy. You know' — Charlie Tingster looked after Claire Shaw as she was carried off, shaking his head — 'like I said, funny old world ain't it?'

★　★　★

Moving through the crowd, Fred's excitement at the prospect of killing the auburn-haired woman grew, until she waved to a man, a uniformed copper, who came and kissed her. After a moment they both looked back and laughed, obviously at the idiot she had told off. His prize snatched from him, Fred came up short, his rage an inferno inside of him.

'Roses again, luv?'

Fred looked to his left to a flower stall, and the familiar Liverpudlian stall-holder. She was looking at him curiously. His concentration on the woman had been so intense, that he had not noticed his closeness to the stall. The woman had remembered him from his previous visit. He would have preferred if she had not recognized him, but he had to accept that he could not hope not to be recognized as his visits would be regular and his request special.

'All right, luv?' she enquired. 'You look a bit off colour, if you don't mind me saying so,' she added quickly.

He rubbed his forehead. 'Headache.'

'Terrible, headache is,' she sympathized. 'My Sam gets them awful migraines. Lays him low, they do.'

Fred smiled charmingly. 'Please. Red roses, yes.'

'Lucky woman,' said the stall-holder. 'My old man wouldn't know what red roses was for if they hit him in the gob!' She laughed. 'Thinks St Valentine is the patron saint of mechanics.' She hunched her shoulders. 'That's Sam Foster for you.'

Fred smiled, even more charmingly.

'I'm not sure that she'd agree that she's a lucky woman,' Fred said.

'Get away. She'll not kick you out of her bed, that's for sure, luv.'

'I'll take that bunch,' Fred said, pointing to a bunch of vivid red roses, the same as the ones he had chosen on his last visit. He needed just a single rose, but asking for just one might make him more memorable if questions were asked. He hated flowers. He'd

79

have to dump the remainder, and waste maddened him. Unless, he thought, he threw caution to the wind and went on a right old killing spree. 'And you'll do the needy, right?'

'Of course, luv,' the woman agreed. 'What is it you want to say this time?'

'Oh, the same as before.'

'*Fred. Kisses.* Right?'

'Yes.'

The woman had a very good memory. And that troubled Fred.

'Simple. But says it all, don't it?'

The woman got a card. She called her husband to write the message on it, and attached it to the roses. 'There ya go, luv.'

'Thanks.'

Fred paid for the roses and walked off, smelling the flowers.

'Nice bloke,' the woman commented to her husband. 'You'd never think he couldn't read or write, would you.'

Overhearing the conversation, but pretending not to, Fred smiled secretly. It was a good yarn he had spun the woman to get the first card written. He was pleased with the idea that when the coppers burnt the midnight oil deciphering the handwriting, he'd have sent them on a wild goose chase.

As he left the Grey's Quay market, Fred knew that shortly he would have to do two things: find another florist. And murder the stall-holders. What else could he do? How long would it be before the police began to check on red roses? And how long would it be before the newspapers would find out, and begin writing about the Rose Killer.

It was a good bet that that would be what they would call him.

'Nice bloke?' scoffed Sam Foster. 'Gives me the heebie-jeebies, he does. Somethin' 'bout him I don't like, Lil.'

'You just don't know what romance is, do you, Sam Foster?' Lil Foster complained.

7

'Did Claire Shaw ever say where she was from?' Lukeson enquired of Tingster.

'Manchester.'

'Are you sure about that?'

'Yeah. Kinda stuck in me mind, her bein' a 'Pool supporter. I mean you'd have expected her to be a United or City supporter, wouldn't ya? And she wasn't from the 'Pool, and that's for sure. Didn't talk funny like the Puds do. Come to think of it, she didn't talk like the Mannies either. She talked like one of them upper-class birds,' Tingster said. 'Like them prats from Eton or Oxford.'

He chuckled, with the leery nod-and-wink of a latter day Sid James on seeing the delicious and delightful Barbara Windsor in a *Carry On* film.

'I remember saying to Frank, Mellor that is, if he kept her on, the bloody forecourt would be chockful in no time with Rollers and Bentos.'

'If he kept her on?' Sally Speckle queried. 'Why, if Claire Shaw was packing the forecourt, would Mellor want to let her go?'

'His WMD wasn't happy, was she.'

82

'His WMD?'

'Weapon of Mass Destruction,' Charlie Tingster explained. 'Frank's other half. Don't know why all them blokes was muckin' about in Iraq. If they was lookin' for a WMD, she was right here on their doorstep.'

'Mrs Mellor was unhappy?'

'Flaming mad as a queen bee after her honey's been nicked.'

'Why was that?' the DI enquired.

'Well, Frank's a bit of a lad, ain't he? Always lookin' for an opportunity, that's our Frank. And Claire Shaw was one hell of an opportunity.'

'Mr Mellor attempted an assignation, then?'

'A what?' Tingster asked, bemused. 'Can you be arrested for that?'

'Tried to get together with Claire Shaw?' Lukeson said patiently.

Speckle was none too pleased with Andy Lukeson's wry grin.

'I'd say. Frank was tryin' to get in her knickers from the second he laid eyes on her. Can't say that I blame him neither.'

'Did Mellor get the opportunity he was looking for?' Lukeson asked.

'Naw. Just a grope among the figrolls.'

'Fact? Or what Frank said?'

'Said.'

'Did you believe him, Mr Tingster?'

'Reckon I did at that, mate,' Charlie Tingster said, after due consideration. 'Frank Mellor's a horny toad, but I never caught him out in no lie.'

'Did you seek an opportunity?' Speckle enquired.

Unabashed, Charlie Tingster admitted, 'O' course I did. A bloke would have to be at least three days dead not to have tried.'

'And what was Ms Shaw's reaction?'

'Said she'd rather kiss dog turd.'

'Did that upset you?'

'Naw. I'm a realist. I ain't no George Clooney, am I?'

Tight, curly ginger hair, small narrow eyes, and a nose that could serve as a site for a mobile phone mast. Charlie Tingster was indeed a realist, Speckle thought.

'Anyone else, that you know of, *try it on*?' Lukeson questioned.

'I'm sure plenty did, but she wasn't havin' any.' Tingster snorted. 'Too high and mighty for the likes of us round here, she was.' There was a sudden and surprisingly vitriolic spite in his voice that, were it to turn to anger, would be a rage that might be unstoppable in its intensity, Lukeson reckoned. 'Like I told ya, Claire Shaw was only offerin' to some bloke who'd be able to give loans to the Bank of England.'

Tingster laughed, but there was no humour in his laughter. It was purely perfunctory, designed, Speckle thought, to put back in hiding the much more sinister side of his nature that had briefly flashed to life.

'Frank Mellor can't have been short of a bob or two,' Lukeson observed. 'That forecourt and shop is a busy place.'

'Frank ain't no pauper, for sure, but neither did he have the kind of dosh Claire Shaw was lookin' to get her hands on.'

'Do you know if she succeeded in getting her wish? That she found this cash-rich man she was looking for?'

'Reckon she did, an' all. She packed in the NHS coupla months ago.' Lukeson's raised eyebrow became a question mark. 'Claire and me's got somethin' . . . had somethin' in common,' he corrected. 'Dodgy waterbags.' And in response to Speckle's puzzlement, clarified: 'Kidneys. When she was at Mellors, we used to meet up at the renal clinic at the hospital. Then suddenly she wasn't there no more. Asked a nurse she was chummy with, said that she'd gone private at some posh clinic near Brigham. So I reckon she hooked Mr Moneybags, 'cause places like that don't come cheap, do they?

'Upped and left right in the middle of a shift, sudden like, she did. Hoppin' mad, was

85

Frank.' Tingster sniggered. 'He'd busted his balls, and figured that he was real close to reapin' the benefits. Pissed off good and proper, he was. Said that if he got his hands on her he'd . . . '

'He'd what?' Lukeson pressed the suddenly reticent Charlie Tingster, who displayed the unease of a man who unwittingly had said too much. 'He'd what?' Lukeson demanded to know.

'Frank's not a bad bloke. Runs off at the mouth a bit — '

'Answer the sergeant's question,' Speckle said tersely. 'I'm waiting, and I don't intend to wait for very long, Mr Tingster.' She let her gaze go towards PC Smith to convey the impression that, were he to delay much longer, Tingster would find himself in custody. She really had no grounds to follow up on her bluff, but she hoped to fool Tingster into thinking she had.

Quick to understand, PC Smith was ready to play his part in his superior's deception for the greater good. His face became officially grim and very convincing. Andy Lukeson thought that Smith might indeed one day be *spotted*.

Convinced that he was on the verge of trouble, Tingster blurted out, 'Frank said that if he got his hands on her he'd wring her neck. But he didn't mean nothin' by it. If you ask me, Claire Shaw didn't just up and leave. I think that, with Frank away at a relative's funeral in Leeds, his WMD grabbed her chance to give Claire the push.

'Hated Miss High-and-mighty's guts, she did. Give Claire a dose of snake venom. That's what Sarah Mellor said.'

'You heard her say that?'

'Yeah, but she don't know I did.'

'Then how did you hear her say it?' Speckle asked.

'Went round to the house to touch Frank for a coupla quid. They were havin' an argy-bargy about Frank chasin' Claire Shaw. That's when I heard his WMD. I wasn't eavesdroppin'. I reckon half the bleedin' county heard. Mrs M's got mighty lungs when she's on a rant.'

'When did you *accidentally* overhear this?' Lukeson enquired. 'Might it be around the time Claire Shaw left Mellors' employment?'

'Yeah. A coupla days before. Frankie boy told the missus that he'd drop her like a hot potato if Claire Shaw gave him the nod.'

Lukeson thought, hatred and frustration were strong motives for murder, and when it came to the Mellors they were shared emotions, but the Mellors did not fit in with the current theory that Fred was connected in some way to the Loston Mental Hospital. Of course, that was an assumption and not, as yet a proven fact.

'Do you know if Mellor is in any way connected with Loston Mental Hospital?' he enquired of Tingster.

'The mento? Never heard 'im say so, but Sarah Mellor is.'

'Mrs Mellor?'

'Yeah. She's on some charity that visits. Had a schizo brother who topped himself. Doin' her bit an' all that.'

The glance that Speckle shot Lukeson showed that her thoughts were at one with his. 'Do you have any connection with the mental hospital, Mr Tingster?' Lukeson asked.

'Don't even go past it,' he snorted. 'All them nutters runnin' abou', lookin' for someone to top. Don't be daft.'

'So Claire Shaw found Mr Right, then?' Speckle said.

'Fell on her feet for sure. The next time me and Claire's paths crossed, she was wearin' designer gear instead of the shabby off-the-peg stuff she used to tog out in. And she drove a spankin' new motor, too. With all o' that, added to her treatment at a posh private clinic and a posh house, it don't take a genius to figure out that she'd landed the big fish she'd been slingin' her hook for.'

Tingster shrugged philosophically.

'If ya've got what Claire Shaw had, ya might as well make it work for ya, right?'

'Do you know where Claire Shaw lived now?' Lukeson asked.

'Naw.'

'And Jack Ansome?'

'Probably on some street corner rantin' and ravin' about damnation, I shouldn't wonder,' Tingster scoffed. 'A right nutter, he was. Fit bugger, was Ansome. Used to hoist a friend of his, Benny Frederics, who was no weaklin', on to his shoulders as if he was tissue paper. It was Ansome's party trick.'

He chuckled.

'Musta been all that sloggin' through the bush, eh.'

'And Frederics?'

'He could be anywhere. He chucked porterin' at the mento a coupla months ago.'

'Frederics worked at the mental hospital?' Speckle queried.

'Yeah. Used to fill in at weekends, and when a porter would go on the sick. And who'd blame them, shufflin' nutters round all day long. Used to say that if he could, he'd lock Claire Shaw up with the nutters and throw 'way the key. Make the posh bitch suffer, he said.'

'Why was that?' Lukeson asked.

'One night, like the rest of us did at one time or another, he chanced his luck with her. Never heard what she said to Frederics, but I reckon that he'd have gladly cut her up into little pieces and flushed her down the loo, so flamin' mad he was.'

'What did Ansome think of Claire Shaw?'

'Ansome never said nothin'.' Charlie Tingster shrugged. 'But if looks could kill . . . '

'It seems Claire Shaw rubbed people up the wrong way,' Speckle said.

'She was a toffee-nosed cow. Plain and simple.'

'Did Ansome ever mention what order of missionaries he'd been in?'

'Don't think so.'

'You've been most helpful, Mr Tingster,' Sally Speckle said.

'We must all help the police do their job, right?'

'Wouldn't we wish that everyone was so civic minded. You mentioned that you were keeping an eye on the place for Mr Tattan. You live nearby, then?'

Tingster pointed due west. 'Just round the next bend. Yellow house. Can see the place from my bedroom window. I'd have been here a lot sooner, only I was havin' a bit of a kip. Sometimes my dodgy waterbags give me gyp and I have to rest.'

'That must be tedious for you,' Speckle sympathized. 'An old derelict building like this must attract a lot of undesirables. See anyone hanging round of late, Mr Tingster?'

'The odd tramp. It's a bit off the beaten track.'

'When were you here last to check?' Lukeson enquired.

'Nothin' to check is there? I cast an eye now and then. Archie was payin' me at first, but the funds dried up. So no pay, no way, I say.' Obviously tiring of being questioned, he enquired, 'That it, then?'

'For now, Mr Tingster,' Speckle said.

'What d'ya mean for now?' he protested.

'Sometimes we find that people overlook some little thing that could help us a lot when recalled.'

'Should've minded me own business!' Tingster said sourly, and stormed off.

Her mood thoughtful, Speckle went to the door. Tingster was at the far side of what used to be the car-park, but was now an overgrown area of disintegrating tarmac. Several constables were searching the area.

'Fred!' she called out.

'Yes, ma'am,' a young fresh-faced rookie responded, obviously mystified as to why he should have been summoned.

'Nothing,' the DI said.

Tingster had not made the slightest response to her summons that she could see. Killers, particularly the kind of sick pervert who called himself Fred liked to get close to the scene of crime, and often actually insinuated themselves into it.

'It always works in the movies,' she said to Andy Lukeson, when he joined her.

'You've heard Fred. Does Tingster sound anything like him? He is pretty distinctive.'

Sally Speckle shook her head. 'Fred was . . . well spoken.'

'Jack Ansome would have had a seminary education,' Lukeson said. 'I reckon it would be nigh on impossible for Tingster, even watching every word, to be gaffe free for five seconds,' he opined.

'You're ruling Tingster out, then?'

'I never rule anyone in or out,' Lukeson said. 'I've been bitten on the arse too many times. Tingster would have us believe that he took Shaw's rejection in his stride. She'd rather kiss dog turd, she said. That would be a pretty heavy blow to any man's ego, the kind of thing that could fester. He lives right on the doorstep of the crime scene, he's familiar with it and been charged with minding it. And he knew Benny Frederics, who was a part-time porter at the mental hospital — that's a link to the hospital.'

'A tenuous link, Andy.'

'Agreed, but still a link. And Ansome also had the same link.'

'How could Tingster or Ansome have possibly known about the CCTV being upgraded to enable them to carry out his plan to phone me? Frederics is no longer working at the hospital to tell either of them.'

DS Andy Lukeson grinned. 'Don't expect me to have all the answers. I'm only a sergeant.'

Sally Speckle laughed.

'Cheeky sod! Sarah Mellor was a surprise, Andy. Being on a visiting charity, she'd have a knowledge of what goes on at the mental hospital. There's a good chance that she'd have known about the ugrading of the CCTV.'

'But she's not male. And, I doubt if she'd give Tingster, Frederics or Ansome the time of day, let alone insider knowledge.'

'She might have given it to her husband though,' Sally Speckle said sombrely. 'Better assemble the team, Andy.'

'Already in hand, boss.'

DI Sally Speckle looked into the premature gloom of the evening. 'He's out there somewhere, Andy,' she said soulfully. 'And I have this creepy feeling that he's already arranging another present for me.'

8

Fred found himself back at the park. A drizzle was falling, but he did not mind mist. He liked its silence and its secrecy. It gave him a sense of invisibility. Mist had a quietness and mystery that rain did not have, and he liked its cobwebby feel on his face.

As he strolled through the park, he wondered if anyone had done research on murders in mist. Were there more or fewer murders on misty days? He'd bet that there were more. Mist, he felt, had a seductive quality that induced evil. He had always imagined that the shifting swirls of mist were really shape-changers, demons that crept up and whispered in one's ear, coaxing people to be their human agents of evil. He made a mental note to go online to check if there had been any research done.

In the mist he was a predator; the lion in the long grass; the Ripper in the London fog, moving silently, watching, waiting, pouncing. That made him feel so alive. Made him feel so powerful. So sexually potent. And the closer he got to his victim, the greater that sexual potency became until breath-taking relief exploded from within him and he had a sense of being totally free and floating like some pagan God of vengeance to be feared and glorified. And gloriously, divinely breathless to the point of extinction; an extinction he would not hesitate to embrace if the rush of blood, the heightened senses, the tensing of muscle and the tremble of bone and sinew lasted for even a second longer. But then when he did not reach the ultimate relief, he felt cheated. The angry blood sang in his ears, filling his head until it squeezed against his skull and replaced pleasure with pain. Later, he felt himself cast into a place of darkness, a place of sinister scratchings, like the scratchings in the darkness under the stairs where his stepfather had locked him for a whole day and night, naked, when he had caught him doing something naughty in his bedroom. Fred remembered feeling the soft brush of fur against his skin, and he would see the bright spots of light in the darkness, and see the small yellow teeth bared, and the awful sweep of a rat's tail across his face just as he came from sleep, and often the warm dribble of the rodent's urine, and he would scream for deliverance, for mercy. Then when his screams went unanswered, would come the whimpering. Piteous, defeated whining. And then came the pleading, but no one came, not even his mum. She was drunk, of course, but even drunk, could she not hear his cries. He was convinced that she could, but that she didn't care. He hated her, hated her with an intensity that burned inside him in an inferno of rage as hot as hell and, like hell fire, could not be put out. She had cheated on him. She had married another man when his father had died, after promising that she would not. And had then told him that the reason for bringing that awful pig Bert Stratton into their lives was his need for a father, when what she had really wanted was . . .

He had listened at their bedroom door.

Not all women, of course, were cheats, but a lot were, women such as Claire Shaw. Sarah Worth, Alistair Worth's wife was, he had observed, a good wife and a caring mother. Yet Claire Shaw had not cared. She had lured Alistair into her bed, and did not care a fig about the hurt she would cause Sarah Worth.

Claire Shaw had been a whole lot like his mother. A cheat. A rotten cheat. A filthy whore!

Fred smiled. It was clever, what he had done: putting Bert Stratton's van in reverse gear and crushing his mother against the wall. At twelve years old, it had been called a 'horrible accident'. His grin widened. The drizzle and mist was thickening.

The more dense it became, the better he liked it.

Fred changed direction and strolled along the path where, earlier that afternoon, he'd set the duck on fire. He saw the woman he had seen before coming towards him, still walking her poodle, wearing a dreadful pink raincoat. He went past. She glanced at him warily, and did a quick check on who else might be around. There was no one else. As he passed, he had a mischievous urge to go boo, but he curbed his impulse. He walked on, putting on a show of complete indifference. He could feel her eyes on him, after a slowing of her steps. She was watching him. Maybe *she* fancied him, he thought. Probably compulsively walking the poodle to cope with a hormonal crisis. He walked on, but at a safe distance slowed and turned. The woman was almost lost in the mist which was thickening to fog. She would have become invisible, if it were not for the pink raincoat she was wearing.

Fred decided to follow her.

★ ★ ★

DI Sally Speckle put up a photograph of the battered Claire Shaw before the assembled team, the exception being Sue Blake who,

97

having decided to do a course in Social Studies, had sought temporary secondment as a Community Officer on a council estate afflicted with anti-social behaviour aplenty and known to the police as Asboland. She'd gone to Clewbridge to get work experience. However, rumour round the station favoured the view that having got inadvisedly entangled with PC Brian Scuttle, whose marriage had been in trouble, Blake's sudden interest in social behaviour had more to do with getting out of the way, than concern for the social problems of the notorious Clew.

'What kind of a monster did that?' said DC Helen Rochester, cringing on seeing the photograph of the battered woman.

'The kind who should be locked away, and not in a comfy hospital either with every comfort laid on,' PC Brian Scuttle said sourly. 'Should be put down for the animal he is.'

'Objectivity, Brian,' Speckle said. 'Remember the golden rule. We catch: the courts punish.'

Scuttle shot her a sullen look.

'He'll probably be tried by a liberal bleeding-heart judge, who'll spout a lot of crap about reform and rehabilitation and why this bastard should get a chance to rebuild his life, and his victim, or probably *victims*, won't get a mention.'

Speckle thought about restating the role of the police, but to do so would only add to the tension that Scuttle's trenchant views — not uncommon views in the police, who had to labour at the coalface of crime — had generated. Instead, she wisely paused for a short spell to let the dust settle. Straightening out Scuttle was now a top priority. He had domestic and personal problems he needed to deal with swiftly because, though she was sympathetic, as a senior officer hunting a brutal killer her sole concern had to be for the overall effectiveness of that hunt and its successful conclusion.

'Right. Here's what we have,' she said. 'The victim is aged late twenties to early thirties. At present, based on a preliminary ID by one Charlie Tingster, by means of a tattoo and a name on the victim's dressing-gown, the dead woman's name was Claire Shaw. We believe that the victim suffered from kidney disease, again info by Tingster which will be determined in the post-mortem and will firm up the victim's ID. No fingerprints and no DNA on file. That leaves dental records.'

She addressed DC Charlie Johnson.

'Check Loston and Brigham dentists, Charlie. Alec Balson spotted a recent filling in a right-sided wisdom tooth, which suggests that it might have been done round here, although she was not from these parts, Manchester we believe.'

'Tingster?' Rochester enquired. Speckle nodded. 'Cooperative sort, our Charlie.'

★ ★ ★

The thickening fog made it necessary for Fred to quicken his pace, but he had to be careful, fog was unpredictable, it could shift suddenly and spoil everything.

He liked to follow women to watch the movement of their bodies, his mind full of what he would like to do to them. Even as a boy, he liked to follow women. On his way home from school, on the day his stepfather had caught him in his bedroom doing that naughty thing, he had followed a woman, and had his mind not been full of her and the mould of her small but perfectly shaped bottom against lycra pants, he would not have been caught off guard. He had blamed (and still did) that woman for his time under the stairs. He had grown to hate her. Only for her jiggling bum, he would not have got into trouble.

For a time after he gave up following women, and vowed that he would never again do so. However, he was drawn back to them, but in a different way. Yes, he still desired

100

them, but he also wanted to hurt them — hurt them terribly, as he had done to Claire Shaw. That dark desire had grown and grown and was still growing.

As a boy, he had longed for manhood, when he would possess all the women he could possibly want. But as he grew from boy to man, he realized he did not want to risk their laughing at him, as his mum had laughed when Bert Stratton had explained why he was putting him under the stairs. Once he reached manhood, Fred decided that he would have women, yes, but they would not be able to laugh at him — never that — never again.

★   ★   ★

DI Speckle continued, 'As you can see from the photograph, there was a great deal of anger in the killer to have done what he did. The weapon, as yet not found, is probably a poker — Alec Balson's educated guess.'

'Body dumped at the former and now derelict Old Mill pub, a forensics nightmare. So if any help comes from that quarter it will be slow in arriving. Dead about twelve hours, which puts her time of death at about two a.m. this morning, give or take either side.'

'We have no idea where she was murdered.'

★   ★   ★

Some women Fred tired of, and did not follow for long. Others . . . well, there was something about them that drew him like a filing to a magnet. That's the way it had been with Claire Shaw. For a time it seemed that she had wanted him as much as he her. Then, when he had got up the courage to tell her how he felt, she had laughed. 'Don't be silly,' she had said, and had laughed all the more. He had wanted to kill her then and there, and it would have been so easy to do. Everything was at hand. It would probably have gone down as a mistake, an unfortunate accident. However, another idea had come to him out of the blue, as some of the best ideas can. He would kill Claire Shaw (as a start) and tease the woman he had hated for so long — Detective Inspector Sally Speckle. Kill two birds with the one stone, he had thought amusedly. Hurt Shaw, and ruin Speckle. It was, he had decided, the perfect plan. And now that he had begun, well, the whole thing was open ended.

★   ★   ★

Despite her overwhelming compulsion to look behind her, the woman resisted the urge.

102

Were she to do so, and then see the man following her, he might pick up all the wrong signals. Though he had feigned indifference, she had sensed his interest in her. Or had that been her ego falsely flattering her at a time when she needed to feel good about herself? This was possible as she had just ended a relationship with a man whose faults she, and no one else, had been stupidly blind to.

The mist had thickened to fog, making the park an alien landscape from which she longed to escape. She could hear the rumble of traffic, but instead of comforting her its noise only heightened her sense of isolation and aloneness. New to the area, it was only her third visit to the park, and two of those had been within hours of each other, so the topography of the place was unknown to her. She knew the entrances and exits, but her fear now was that in her anxiety she would branch off on to one of the less frequented paths — paths overhung by murky trees, with a plethora of bushes and shrubbery that made perfect hiding places for the ill-intentioned.

Where had everyone suddenly disappeared to? They were probably still around, but unlike her were wearing rubber-soled walking shoes or trainers.

She wondered how close the man was to her?

The park had two gates, north and south. She reckoned that she was nearer the south gate, but the north gate was nearer to her new house, and she so wanted to reach the safety of home. Should she exit the park as quickly as she could by the south gate? Or persevere and go on to the north?

Should she continue to walk? Or should she run!

★   ★   ★

'Her killer has a name, which he has kindly given to me.' All eyes turned on Speckle. 'He calls himself Fred.' She brought them up to speed on the events of that morning.

'Creep,' WPC Anne Fenning said.

'Anne has also had the dubious pleasure of having spoken to Fred,' Speckle explained. 'Probably not his actual name, of course. He likes to give me what he calls presents. Claire Shaw was his first present, and it's reasonable to assume that unless we catch him quickly there will be others. It is also reasonable to assume that it's probably something in my past that has brought Fred out of the woodwork. Or he's simply a sadistic nutter. Why now, I don't know. Maybe Fred needed time to work up courage, or maybe it's simply that his budding paranoia has now become fullblown insanity.'

'Fred first phoned from a payphone in the reception at Loston Mental Hospital. A witness, Rupert Shooter, saw a man making a call about the time I received Fred's call. The man was wearing one of the distinctive green dressing-gowns worn by patients involved in the hydrotherapy programme.'

'Hold on,' Charlie Johnson said. 'If he's a patient, he wouldn't be out and about murdering women.'

'Exactly, Charlie,' Speckle said.

'So it was someone wearing a patient's robe as a disguise,' Rochester said.

'Probably to cover up clothing that would identify the caller,' Speckle said. 'Medical staff? Or service staff with distinctive work clothes, maybe bearing a logo or a service provider's name.'

'But there would be CCTV,' Rochester said. 'In a mental hospital it must be everywhere.'

'CCTV was not working. It's being upgraded at the moment.'

'This bloke's a planner,' Charlie Johnson said. 'Well organized. Murders Shaw at two a.m. knowing that he could safely phone you this morning from the payphone because the CCTV would not be working.'

★   ★   ★

The woman thought she saw movement behind a tree to the right of the path up ahead. The man probably knew the park well and had got ahead of her. Her step faltered. Classic Hitchcock, she thought. Keep going and walk into trouble. Or turn back and walk into trouble. By now the audience would know which was safe and which was not, and would probably be shouting out the way in which to go.

Perhaps it was a trick of the fog?

Unable to quell her curiosity a moment longer, she turned round. There was no one there. The man had not followed her after all. A labrador ambled out from behind the tree up ahead, and started the poodle barking. Taking a couple of deep breaths to ease her tension, the woman continued on.

No hurry now.

★ ★ ★

'So we're looking for Fred among the hospital staff?'

'Probably, Charlie,' Speckle said. 'But there are other possibles, and chief among those is a man called Benny Frederics. Frederics used to work as a porter at the mental hospital, so he'd know the hospital's routines. And, apparently Claire Shaw was not very nice to him. In fact, it appears that she had not been nice to anyone whom she considered to be a lesser mortal.'

'Sounds like a right bitch,' Helen Rochester said. 'The perfect candidate for murder.'

'Worked at the mental hospital, ma'am, you said?' Johnson questioned. 'How long ago?'

'Up to a couple of months ago. Hospitals, like all big organizations, tend to stick with what works. So the likelihood is that the hospital still functions as it did when Frederics worked there. And as a porter, he'd have intimate enough knowledge of the hospital to be able to move around with confidence. He'd know where to pick up a patient's dressing-gown, I'd imagine.'

'And Frederics' motive?' Rochester asked.

'Hatred and revenge, plain and simple. Like others, he tried it on with Claire Shaw. Got the boot. And was fit to cut her into little pieces and flush her down the loo.'

'Tingster?' Rochester queried.

'Tingster,' Speckle confirmed. 'Are you getting a hang up on him, Helen?'

'I just feel that he's been a little too ready to co-operate, guv. Always suss, isn't? People usually head the other way when a copper shows up.'

'Now we come to Jack Ansome, a general dogsbody at the Old Mill. Before they fell out, Ansome and Frederics were friends. So it's reasonable to assume that Frederics would have talked about his job at the mental hospital. And it's also reasonable to assume that Ansome might have visited Frederics at the hospital.'

'And Ansome's motive?' Johnson asked.

'Possibly one even more deadly than Frederics: religious righteousness. He might have seen Shaw as a scarlet woman — '

'How?' WPC Anne Fenning questioned. 'If Shaw was giving the boot to every man who tried, that would make her a saint, not a scarlet woman.'

'It was well known that had the right man come along, one with lots of dosh, she wouldn't have been so saintly. That might have even made her worse in Ansome's eyes. And who knows, maybe his desire for Shaw, clashing with his religious mania might have been a conflict he'd have preferred to rid himself of by removing the object that was causing him to sin, in thought if not in deed. Maybe to a man like Ansome, a former priest, there was no difference between the two.'

★   ★   ★

Fred stood stock-still against the oak tree he had taken cover behind seconds before,

108

instinctively sensing that the woman was going to turn round; it had been a close call. A sudden breeze had punched a hole in the fog, and for a hair-raising moment he had been clearly visible. How long should he wait? Too soon and he'd be rumbled; too long, she'd be lost in the fog and he'd be cheated of his prize.

He'd count to ten, as he had always done as a boy when a decision needed to be made.

★   ★   ★

'Frederics and Ansome both worked at the Old Mill pub where Claire Shaw was found, Ansome full-time, and Frederics as a casual. So we have two suspects linked to each other, to the place where the body was dumped, and to the location from where Fred phoned,' Lukeson said. 'They were friends until Judy Mayhew, the barmaid at the Old Mil, became an issue. Ansome, a former priest still on a mission, was still saving souls and saw lust as the route to damnation. Frederics told him to get stuffed.'

'A religious nutter,' Scuttle said. 'Always dodgy, religious nutters.'

'Did Ansome pack it in? Or was he booted out?' Johnson asked.

'I'm waiting on a Father Lake to come

back to me with the story,' WPC Anne Fenning said.

'What about CCTV, Andy?' Rochester questioned. 'How would Frederics or Ansome know that it was being upgraded and not working?'

'Possibly by still being in contact with someone working at the hospital,' Speckle said. 'An old mate. It could simply have come up in conversation as a kind of grouse about having extra work with the CCTV down. And, if Frederics is Fred, he was looking a gifthorse in the mouth and acted.'

'And finally we need to look at Tingster, Frank and Sarah Mellor.'

'Sarah's a woman,' Scuttle snorted.

'Very observant,' Andy Lukeson said, tersely responding to Scuttle's *what kind of an idiot have we here* manner. 'But if you have nothing else to do, or nowhere else to go, bear with me, Constable.'

The reference to Scuttle's official rank, rather than the normal informality of team briefings, initiated an air of discipline rather than the usual camaraderie that was the hallmark of such gatherings. It was to be regretted. Lukeson reckoned that Scuttle was allowing his personal problems to dominate his attitude, however, and with Charlie Johnson's long standing gripe about Sally Speckle's decison to make Helen Rochester his replacement when he was away on a course, a big stick approach was warranted to get priorities right.

'Doesn't make sense, that's all,' Scuttle said, poutily.

'Probably not, Brian,' Lukeson said, easing off a little on the pedal of discipline. 'But humour your old sarge, eh. Ma'am, the floor is yours.'

'Shaw worked for the Mellors at their service station,' Speckle continued. 'But Frank Mellor had a wider view of service than just stacking the shelves and operating the checkout which, naturally enough, Sarah Mellor didn't agree with. One day, when Mellor was away in Leeds at a family funeral, Shaw upped and left. Mellor was hopping mad and, according to one Charlie Tingster — '

'Him again,' DC Helen Rochester groaned.

'Mellor said that if he set eyes on Shaw, he'd wring her neck. So maybe he battered her to death instead.'

'Now the interesting thing is,' Sally continued, 'that Sarah Mellor is involved in a charity that visits the mental hospital. According to Tingster, her brother was a schizophrenic who committed suicide. Thus we have a link to the hospital for both Mellors.'

'And Tingster?' Johnson enquired, in a less combative manner.

'He had, by his own admission, tried it on with Shaw. That she'd rather kiss dog turd, had been her response.'

'That was a right kick in the balls,' Scuttle said, also in a less griping manner, Lukeson was pleased to note.

'Having got the heave-ho from Shaw in a manner befitting a lice-ridden dog, Tingster might have had the same motive as Frederics,' Speckle said. 'Hatred and revenge. He was caretaker of sorts where the body was dumped. However, he doesn't own a vehicle. So how could he have got Shaw's body from wherever she was murdered to where she was dumped?'

'An accomplice with a motor?' WPC Anne Fenning suggested, but not convincingly.

'I don't think so, Anne,' Speckle opined. 'For one thing, I reckon Fred is a loner.'

'So is that Tingster out of the frame, then?' DC Helen Rochester asked.

'He could have got a loan of a car,' Scuttle said. 'Or hired one.'

'Possibly,' Lukeson agreed. 'But like the boss, I think Fred is a loner. Getting a loan of a car would mean someone out there could drop him in it. And, though Charlie Tingster is not the brightest bulb on the Christmas tree, I think he'd tumble to the idea that if he hired a car we'd find it and get forensics to go over it.'

'A second point against Tingster being the killer, is how would he have known that the hospital CCTV was not functioning? He says that he has no idea where Frederics or Ansome are. Sarah Mellor could possibly have told him, but why would she? Even if she knew, it's not something that pops up in casual conversation. '*Hey, by the way, the CCTV will not be working at the hospital on X day*'. In fact I doubt very much if Sarah Mellor would give Tingster the time of day.'

'And even if she volunteered the information, or Tingster wheedled it out of her, why would he want to, because it was not something he could plan around? The fact that the CCTV was down could only help an opportunist. And that still leaves the problem of moving around the hospital with the degree of freedom that would allow Tingster to get his hands on a patient's dressing-gown.'

'Personally, I think Tingster as a suspect is an outsider. However, there always remains the possibility that Tingster is a lot more intelligent that I'm giving him credit for.'

★　★　★

'I won't let that brute harm you Truffles,' the woman reassured the poodle when he began to bark, thinking that it was the Labrador that

113

had caused it to be anxious.

'Shut it, you little turd,' Fred growled. The tree was not one of those great oaks that an army could be hidden behind, as great oaks went it was not much more than a sapling, and all it would take to be discovered was for the woman to backtrack a little. When the poodle continued to bark, he promised grimly, 'You're for the microwave when I get my hands on you.' But at least the poodle had one use, and that was that its bark helped him to judge the distance and the location of the woman. She was static.

That was worrying.

Unperturbed by the poodle's barking, the Labrador passed by, but on seeing Fred, it became curious and stopped.

★   ★   ★

'A man called Rupert Shooter saw a man using the payphone,' Speckle said. 'But all he got was an impression of someone muscular, going to seed . . . '

'Not much help, that,' Rochester said.

'If this man is Fred, maybe he used to work out. So a check on gyms might throw something up.'

'Without a description it's pretty hopeless,' Scuttle said.

114

'We can but try, Brian,' Speckle said. 'Now, significantly perhaps, Ansome was described by Tingster as a 'fit bugger', whose party trick was to hoist Frederics, who in Tingster's words was no weakling, on to his shoulders like a piece of tissue paper. That suggests that Ansome would fit Shooter's description of the man using the payphone, if Ansome had let himself go, that is.'

'Tingster on the other hand went to seed a long time ago.'

'Does Shooter work at the hospital?' Johnson enquired.

'Yes. And therefore would know that the CCTV was being upgraded, Charlie.'

'Maybe his *vague impression* of the man using the payphone is because he couldn't describe himself, ma'am.'

'It's a thought,' Speckle said.

'Has Shooter got form?' Rochester asked.

'Squeaky clean,' Lukeson replied.

'Everyone is, before they're nobbled, Sarge.'

'All this cynicism from one so young and lovely,' Lukeson flung back, with a wry grin.

'It's called withdrawal from sticky buns, Sarge.'

★   ★   ★

115

Fred could sense the woman's interest brought on by the Labrador's curiosity. Then he could hear the squelch of her shoes on the wet path coming back towards him.

★ ★ ★

'So far nothing I can see in my past points to a motive for Fred's actions,' Speckle said. 'A theory' — she glanced wryly at Lukeson — 'is that Fred has been *attracted* to me.'

'Maybe that's not as daft as it seems, boss,' DC Helen Rochester said. 'There was that photograph in the *Loston Echo* that made you look like a Hollywood babe on Oscar night.'

'I have it pinned up on the door of my wardrobe,' Andy Lukeson said, evincing a chortle from the team, who would actually not have been surprised if it were true.

'That's what every DI needs. A comedian for a sergeant,' Speckle flung back good-humouredly. 'Another theory might be that, based on past successes, Fred might want to challenge me. See how good I am.'

'It's a game that might appeal to a deranged mind,' Scuttle said. 'A human version of a computer game, eh?'

'Who knows,' Speckle said. 'But at this point it's as legitimate a theory as any other.

Or he might, in his twisted way, really be giving me presents. And, of course, he might be doing this to end my career when I fail to catch him. It may be revenge, I have been involved in some high-profile cases, so therein might lie the motive for all of this.'

★ ★ ★

Alarmed by the prospect of imminent discovery, Fred glanced around him for a means of escape, but there was none. There was a stretch of open grass between him and some bushes on a little hillock, which he would have no hope of reaching unseen.

The squelch of the woman's footsteps was getting ever nearer.

★ ★ ★

'Finally, Andy and I have already spoken to an Alan Harper,' Speckle told them, 'whose phone Fred stole and is using.' She gave her opinion that Harper was not in the running as a suspect. 'And, there's Shooter, of course.' She outlined the gist of Shooter's interview, ending, 'Shooter grows very nice roses, and Fred likes to give me roses. Andy nicked one of them for lab analysis to see if we have a match for the rose Fred so kindly left in my car. Andy, clever lad that he is, reckoned that the roses might prove a match for things like nutrients and pesticides, and also local environmental factors. So, fingers crossed.'

'One thing interesting about Shooter, is that he lives on Allworth Avenue. Now, Shooter, who had his house up for sale has had to withdraw it from the market because of the drop in value after the avenue's high profile in the Pick Up case. Again, Andy, clever — '

'Lad that he is,' the team choroused.

' — has come up with the idea that Shooter's misfortune — '

'Sounds like the title of a ribald seventeenth-century country romp,' WPC Anne Fenning interjected.

' — in not being able to unload his house because of my antics on the avenue, might have put a financial millstone round his neck, and thereby supplying a motive for all of this festering bitterness.'

'A bit off the wall, that,' DC Charlie Johnson opined.

'Perhaps not, if you're a nutter,' Lukeson said.

'Next,' Speckle said, 'is one Larry Brite, who works as a contract cleaner at the mental hospital. Brite's got form for making nasty phone calls to women. He answered when I

118

phoned back the payphone in reception, but, before you get carried away, Brite has an alibi. He was in the hospital administrator's office chasing a mouse. Thomas, the administrator, has confirmed this.'

'Shooter was pretty hostile when Andy and I interviewed him. He refused a sample of his handwriting which I had hoped to compare with the handwriting on the card which accompanied the rose Fred left in my car. His refusal might be significant. Or it might be that he was just being bloody-minded. He's not a very welcoming or co-operative sort.'

'On the other hand, Brite willingly gave us a sample of his handwriting. But it seems to have little if any likeness to Fred's and bears a definite resemblance to the signature we have on file for Brite.'

'With an alibi, why is Brite still in the mix?' WPC Anne Fenning asked.

'There's no good reason,' Sally Speckle said, 'other than he has a track record worth noting, Anne.'

★ ★ ★

Squelch.

Squelch . . .

The woman was getting closer by the second. A description given to the police is not what he wanted. They might not take too much notice of a middle-aged woman reporting a man following her in the park. There were probably a hundred such reports in any given week, most the product of vivid imaginations. Or egos that needed to be stoked, even by imaginary attackers. Such a report would probably be a long way down the police list of priorities. But it would be noted. Everything was noted. And therefore he would exist, whereas now he did not.

Fred had a decision to make. And he had only seconds in which to make it.

★   ★   ★

'Prints have dusted the payphone at the hospital,' Lukeson informed the team, 'but they have only come up with smudges and nothing good enough for a match. The best we can hope for is a partial. Now, if we're considering Shooter as a suspect, he never uses payphones because he has a phobia about germs.'

By agreement with Andy Lukeson, Speckle did not tell the team about Fred's possible intrusion into her home. At first Lukeson had disagreed. She had voiced the opinion that informing the team might open up a spurious line of inquiry which might waste time. If she decided to get SOCO in and they found

120

nothing, because her imagination was working overtime, they would lose precious hours at the opening of the inquiry: the right decisions in those first hours and days made the difference between a killer in the dock and a cold case.

'We don't know, as yet, where Claire Shaw lived,' Andy Lukeson said. 'Mellor should be able to supply that information when I go round.'

'Mellor was trying it on with Shaw,' Fenning said. 'A man with his blood up, can be a very unpredictable animal. Sexual frustration could account for the viciousness of the murder.'

'Put the blood up in many men then, have you?' Scuttle snorted.

'Tosser!'

Speckle had had enough.

'PC Scuttle, I would appreciate constructive discussion not mindless sniping! And' — her attention switched to Fenning — 'though I fully understand your reaction, WPC Fenning, I would ask that all of you confine yourselves to finding Claire Shaw's killer and behave in a manner befitting professional police officers. Is that understood?'

There was a chorous of: 'Ma'am.'

'Now there is one other possibility we should consider,' DS Andy Lukeson said.

'And that is that Fred is a myth.'

'A myth?' Rochester said.

'Let's play that favourite game detectives indulge in when they have a mountain of questions and no answers — the *what if?* game. So what if Claire Shaw's murder is not the work of a deranged mind, but your everyday common murder?'

'You mean a once off, Sarge,' Fenning questioned.

Lukeson nodded. 'A one off, Anne, but our killer creates the smokescreen of a nutter behind which to hide.'

'But that wouldn't work without . . . ' PC Brian Scuttle's expression became grave. 'Without . . . '

'More killings to maintain the illusion of Fred, Brian,' Lukeson said.

'Bloody hell!'

'So while we're gadding about looking for a nutter, the sane-as-can-be murderer is safe. Well, relatively so. Murder is never without risk. Then suddenly the killings stop and we all breathe a sigh of relief that Fred has died or been locked up somewhere. And with no more murders, new cases need solving. Time passes and Fred fades into history.'

'And our killer is safe,' Rochester said.

'Right. So let's not get completely hung up on Fred. Let's keep an open mind. Fred might very well exist, a nutter who likes to murder women, But also think: who among the crop of suspects might be clever enough to have created Fred?'

* * *

Having decided to kill the woman here and now — but disappointed that he had to forego the thrill of the chase — Fred tensed to spring. Fortunately, however the Labrador, alerted by something skittering through the shrubbery on the hillock behind Fred, raced into the bushes. The squelching footsteps paused, and then went in the opposite direction. Fred counted to ten before he edged out from behind the oak. The woman was heading for the north gate. He'd cut across the park to reach it before her.

Arriving at the gate, there was no sign of the woman. After a couple of minutes he began to worry that she had changed her mind, and had chosen to exit the park via the south gate. A sudden panic gripped him.

The loss of the auburn-haired woman at the Grey's Quay market, and now this second prize, worried Fred that his luck had turned bad.

Then he got a glimpse of pink in the fog.

★　★　★

'You're an unlisted number, ma'am,' Johnson said, 'so how did Fred get hold of it?'

DI Speckle told them about Fred's interest in her, and his remark about her new hairdo. 'On my way home after the hairdresser, I called into my local newsagent to order a back number of a magazine I'd missed. As I was leaving, the newsagent asked me for my home phone number to call me when they came in. I called it back to him from the shop door. If Fred was in the shop or nearby, he'd have heard.'

There was one other way, of course, a means she preferred not to dwell on. And that was that Fred had got the number from the phone at her home.

'Has the newsagent CCTV?' Johnson enquired.

'Yes.'

'Worth a look at.'

'I've already checked with Mr Singh. It's a small shop. He re-uses the tape every day. And that's about it for now. Andy will give you your assignments. Thank you all. It's late, so let's call time and get an early and fresh start tomorrow.'

'A word, ma'am?'

'Of course, Charlie. My office.' Closing her

124

office door she immediately said, 'I think I know what this is about. Your request for a transfer, right?'

'Yes, ma'am. It's been three months. DC Allen is leaving. It's a vacancy into which I could fit.'

'Who gets Jack Allen's job is Chief Superintendent Doyle's call.'

'Permission to be frank, ma'am.'

'Say what you feel you need to say, Charlie,' Speckle said.

'I think CS Doyle is sitting on my application for a transfer, thinking that I'll forget about it. I won't,' he stated bluntly. 'And if there's no place here for me, I'll resign and join another force.'

'That's a bit drastic, isn't it? No matter where you go, the Police Force is like Holy Orders. Discipline — absolute discipline is necessary for it to function properly. It's not a bloody democracy. We can't have a ballot every time a decision has to be made. It'll be no different in another force.'

'Have you spoken to CS Doyle recently?'

'Yes, ma'am.'

Doyle's angry voice boomed in Johnson's ears.

'Sally Speckle, unfair? That's a load of old cobblers, Johnson. What might appear to you to be unfair, is Speckle getting the job done

125

as quickly and as efficiently as possible. And I might point out that her track record as a DI is impeccable and spectacular. So we'll have none of this rubbish about her being unfair. Understood?'

'Sir.'

'I'm loath to split up such a fine investigative team,' Doyle had said.

'And?' Speckle asked.

'CS Doyle is not keen, ma'am. And I can only wonder if . . . '

'If?'

'Well, frankly, ma'am, if the CS is taking into account any objections you may have?'

'You think I'm putting the poison in?'

'The thought had crossed my mind, ma'am.'

'I don't want anyone on my team who doesn't want to be there,' Speckle stated brusquely. 'I'll have a word with CS Doyle right now, and make it absolutely clear to him that I think your transfer to DC Allen's vacancy is a good idea. Satisfied?'

'Thank you, ma'am.'

Speckle phoned through to Doyle and made her views known to him. 'Yes, sir.' She handed the phone to Charlie Johnson. 'The CS would like to speak to you.'

'Johnson speaking, sir.' He listened attentively before handing the phone back to Speckle.

126

'I've told Johnson that he can't transfer until the case you're on is successfully concluded,' Doyle told Speckle.

'Was that wise, sir?' Speckle questioned. 'With one eye on the exit, won't Johnson be preoccupied?'

'I don't think so. Charlie Johnson is a very dedicated and focused officer. The decision is made,' Doyle said, when Speckle was of a mind to continue her protest. 'As soon as this fellow who calls himself Fred is nabbed, DC Johnson will fill DC Allen's vacancy. His new guv'nor will be DI Brodders. In the meantime, just get on with it. I don't want to hear of any bouts of handbags in your lot, Sally. With Mulgrave in a uniform that's barely warm on her yet, we don't want to attract her attention too much, now do we?'

'No, sir.'

'Good. What progress is being made in catching this 'Fred'?'

Speckle brought the CS up to speed.

'Not much, is it?' he growled.

'Early days, sir.'

'That's what every copper says when he or she has diddly. Mulgrave is keeping up the pressure, so hopefully we can impress her, Speckle, with a quick arrest.'

'We'll do our best, sir.'

'And hopefully, while you lot are doing

your best, the bastard won't kill again.'

Doyle hung up.

'Fingers crossed, sir,' Speckle said, replacing the phone.

When Johnson left, Andy Lukeson came in. 'How about that birthday drink I promised you?'

'I'm pretty knackered. And I have a rainforest of paperwork to get through that will take several hours. Mind if I give it a miss, Andy?'

'Another time, then.'

'Yes. Another time. Thanks, Andy.'

9

'Mr Mellor?' The man looked up from cleaning the deli equipment. The sudden flash of recognition in Mellor's eyes told Andy Lukeson that Mellor had good instincts, because he had obviously recognized his caller's profession in one fleeting glance. 'DS Lukeson,' he still confirmed nevertheless, 'Loston CID.' Lukeson had been on his way home, but on such a bright late spring evening his flat held no appeal for him, so he had decided to put in an extra hour and call on Frank Mellor.

Frank Mellor was crestfallen. He shot a look further along the shop to where a woman, whom Lukeson presumed was Sarah Mellor, was on one of three busy checkout points. He quickly discarded the food hygiene gloves he was wearing, and tossed them into a pedal waste bin. 'Hate the feel of those things,' he said. 'Make your hands all soft and clammy.' Grabbing Lukeson by the arm, Mellor hurried him along. 'We'll talk in here,' he said, opening the door of a small office to the rear of the shop, pushing Lukeson inside. Mellor went to sit behind the cluttered desk.

He picked up a partially used strip of antacid tablets and crushed it open. 'Peptic ulcer. Is it any bleeding wonder?'

The antacid tablet reminded Lukeson of the indigestion that irregular meals always brought on.

'Wouldn't mind one of those myself,' he said.

'Help yourself.' Lukeson took a tablet and placed the strip back on the desk.

'Keep it.'

'Thanks,' the DS put the antacid tablets in his shirt pocket.

'I'm not exactly clear on why you're here, Sergeant.'

'How well did you know, Ms Shaw, Mr Mellor?'

'She was an employee.'

'Is that all she was?'

'What else?'

DS Andy Lukeson came straight to the point. 'Were you having an affair with Claire Shaw, Mr Mellor?'

'No.' Realizing the false note his denial had struck, Mellor sighed resignedly. 'Have you seen Claire Shaw, Sergeant?'

'Not at her best, Mr Mellor.'

The reason for Mellor's crestfallen reception of Lukeson now became clear.

'Look, has Claire made some kind of

complaint to the police?' he asked. Then, puzzled, 'What do you mean, not at her best?'

Andy Lukeson considered Frank Mellor's last question. If it were a genuine enquiry, it would mean that Mellor thought Shaw was still alive. Of course, he could be a very cunning, quick-thinking man who, given the opportunity to create that impression, had taken it.

He chose to ignore Mellor's question.

'When did you last see Ms Shaw, Mr Mellor?'

'Not since she left here.'

'Spoken to her, have you?'

'A couple of times on the blower.'

'May I ask what about?'

Mellor reacted sharply. 'Is that any of your business? What did Claire say to you lot?'

'Had Ms Shaw grounds for complaint?' Lukeson queried.

'No.' His denial had a breathless quality.

'When she left your employment, why were you trying to contact her again?'

'To get her to come back to work, of course.'

'I'm sure you would not have had a problem replacing Ms Shaw. Unless, of course, you considered her to be irreplace-able?'

'What's that supposed to mean?' Mellor

131

questioned narkily.

Clearly, Mellor was becoming ever more anxious. Lukeson followed his instincts. 'Ms Shaw had grounds for complaint, then, had she, Mr Mellor?' He held Mellor's gaze. 'Sexual harassment, perhaps?'

Mellor paled.

'Might I suggest that the reason you wanted Claire Shaw back had nothing to do with her being an employee, Mr Mellor?' Mellor did not need to answer the question. His averted gaze, and edginess of manner did that for him. 'You said you haven't seen Ms Shaw . . . '

'That's right.'

'But you have tried?'

'Yes.'

'When last did you try, Mr Mellor?'

'I tried to see her last night,' he said, resigned. 'She was due back from a holiday in France. I went round to her place, but there was no one there.'

'What time was that?'

'Latish.'

'What exactly is *latish*, Mr Mellor?'

'About midnight. Half past, maybe.'

'Late for a social call, wasn't it?'

'Not the early to bed type, Claire.'

Alec Balson's estimated time of death put Claire Shaw's murder at 2 a.m, but the time of death as determined scientifically by post-mortem, without the variables attendant at a scene of crime, is more precise and could shift that by an hour or two either way. What if it shifted it towards midnight? There wasn't that great a gap between midnight or half past midnight and 2 a.m. What puzzled Lukeson was Mellor's readiness to admit to visiting Shaw, when the only way the police could have found out he had (barring forensic evidence of his presence) would be if someone had seen him and later on come forward as a witness; that was a long shot that might never materialize. If Mellor was Shaw's murderer, would he not have gambled, kept quiet, in the hope that no one had seen him? However, his line of questioning pertaining to Mellor *having tried* to see Shaw, might have given Mellor the idea that the police already knew about his visit of the previous night. And with a trap set to open, he had opted for disclosure.

'Claire must have been delayed coming back.' Suddenly alarmed, Mellor asked, 'She hasn't been in an accident, has she?'

'Not an accident, no. And she did return from France, Mr Mellor. I'm afraid that Ms Shaw is dead.'

'Dead?'

'Murdered.'

Mellor's shock seemed genuine, but Andy Lukeson had come across murderers before who were good actors.

'In France?' Mellor asked.

The honest question of an innocent man? Or the clever ploy of a murderer, creating an impression of innocence? DS Andy Lukeson wondered.

'Right here in Loston,' Lukeson said, closely observing Frank Mellor. 'Right on your doorstep in fact. Ms Shaw's body was found at the former Old Mill pub.'

Lukeson paused for a beat, his gaze fixed on Mellor.

'You threatened to wring her neck. Did you kill Claire Shaw, Mr Mellor?'

★ ★ ★

As the woman came from the park, Fred joined a bus queue. When she had gone a safe distance, he left the queue and followed her. The fog was nowhere near as dense as it had been in the park, so he was always ready to duck into a doorway or face the other direction if she turned round. The woman turned into a quiet upmarket residential street. He wrote down the name of the street on a piece of a pizza box discarded on a garden wall. Sometimes his memory let him

134

down and he thought it better to note the street name as he had not been all that long in Loston. Halfway along the street, the woman turned into a Victorian original, lovingly maintained except for its sash windows which were pretty far gone and would need replacing soon.

Fred took cover behind a high-sided van parked across the street from the house. The light went on in an upstairs room, her bedroom he suspected. She came to the window and drew the curtains.

'What's your game, then?' Fred swung round. A man was leaning out of a downstairs window of the house behind him, his mood aggressive. 'Go on, then. Piss off!'

Fred hurried away.

★ ★ ★

'Murder Claire,' Frank Mellor wailed. 'No, I did not.'

'I think that's all for now,' Lukeson said. 'We may need to talk to you again, Mr Mellor.'

Frank Mellor's shock had by now turned to anger.

'You should go and talk to the rich ponce Claire's been on her back for,' he barked sourly. 'Pulled in here a couple of times. It was obvious he fancied Claire, and she played him until he was panting. When he was begging for it she hooked him.'

'And he would be?' Lukeson enquired mildly.

'His name's Alistair Worth. Set her up in a house. Posh restaurants. A country hideaway in Norfolk. I hope he's been getting value for money.'

'You took quite an interest in Ms Shaw's comings and goings, didn't you, Mr Mellor?' Andy Lukeson's gaze was steady on him.

'I wasn't stalking her, if that's what you're getting at. I heard things.'

'From whom?'

'A friend of Claire's. A nurse at the renal clinic in Loston General Hospital. Comes in here for petrol. Claire's kidneys weren't the best. Of course, the NHS isn't . . . wasn't,' he amended, 'good enough for Claire anymore. The posh clinic she now goes to in Brigham is much more to that ponce Worth's liking.'

'I'll need Claire Shaw and Worth's addresses.'

'Don't have Worth's.'

He tore a sheet of notepaper on his desk, wrote down Shaw's address and handed it to Lukeson who read it. 'Gladstone Square. A lovenest there would be expensive.' He put the address in his shirt pocket with the strip

136

of antacid tablets Mellor had gifted him.

A man popped his head around the office door. 'Didn't God give you knuckles to knock with?' Mellor bellowed.

Unfazed, the man, dressed in grimy, oil-stained overalls, responded vigorously. 'You should get a dog if you need something to bark.'

'What do you want?' Mellor snapped.

'The station wagon I'm collecting for scrap. Is that it out back? The one with the wing damage and busted headlight?'

'Yes.'

'She ain't a bad motor. You sure you want her scrapped?'

'I wouldn't have phoned you if I didn't. Just take it and go.'

'Not without a hundred quid collection fee, mate. Cash, preferably.'

Frank Mellor handed over a hundred pounds.

'Ta.'

The man left.

'Is that it?' Mellor asked, standing up.

'For now.'

Andy Lukeson followed the scrap merchant out. Walking to his car, he saw the collection truck hoist the station wagon and then drop it in with the rest of the scrapped cars on the truck. Along with the smashed headlight and wing damage, there was a long tear in the passenger door, but nothing that was not repairable in what seemed to be a perfectly serviceable vehicle. He got into the car, started it, and was about to drive away when he braked. Thoughtful, he punched out a number on his mobile. 'Tom, how are things in Traffic?' Tom's answer amused him. 'What you can do for me is, tell me if there was an accident in the region of Gladstone Square last night. Sometime around midnight.' He waited for a moment, then? 'Thanks, Tom. Tell Miriam I said hello.' Lukeson punched out another number. 'DS Andy Lukeson Loston CID. I need a check on . . . ' He turned in the driver's seat to get the registration number of the station wagon and passed it on. He waited. 'Thank you.'

He got out of the car, called out, 'Hold it,' then showed the scrap truck driver his warrant card. 'Drop it down.'

'I can't hang about all day,' he grumbled.

'I'm not asking you to.'

'Fine by me.'

He was getting into the truck when Lukeson said, 'You didn't earn your hundred quid, so I'll take it back to Mr Mellor.'

The man grudgingly handed over the cash. Lukeson sought out Mellor again.

* * *

Changed and relaxed, the woman Fred had been following came back downstairs, poured herself a brandy and sat in front of the sitting-room fire, which she had lit before she had gone to the park. It glowed with a warm invitation to loll. It was late spring with longer evenings promising summer, but still with the chill that warranted a fire. She kicked off her shoes and held the soles of her feet up to the fire, luxuriating in its warmth. The man from the park slipped completely from Assistant Chief Constable Alice Mulgrave's mind.

10

When Mellor saw Lukeson again his shoulders slumped. 'Saw you make a call on your mobile just now.' He nodded to the station wagon. 'An educated guess would be that you were checking up on any accidents in the vicinity of Claire Shaw's house.'

'I might say, Mellor, that that is a very educated guess. But I don't think it's really a guess, is it?'

'It was stupid, I know, but I panicked.' Lukeson waited. 'I was driving back along Bentley Road, that narrow street leading off Gladstone Square, when this git on a bike took a wobble and I hit him. It was his own bloody fault.'

Now Andy Lukeson had a reason for Frank Mellor's earlier forthrightness, and also some explanation for the crestfallen reception he'd received. Mellor had thought that he had come about the accident.

'And you drove off, right?'

'He was up and ranting by the time I reached the end of the street.'

'And a short time later he was in an ambulance. Leaving the scene of an accident is a serious offence, Mellor.'

Lukeson looked at the station wagon, and thought plenty of room in there for Claire Shaw's body. Was that why Mellor had driven off? Was Mellor scrapping the station wagon to destroy trace evidence?

'Why were you driving your wife's car, Mellor?'

'I was having battery trouble.'

'What do you drive?'

'A BMW.'

'Saloon?'

'Yes.'

'New?'

'Six months old. Why?'

Lukeson thought, the station wagon would be a lot roomier to transport a body in. Less expensive and less conspicuous to scrap than a Beamer. And Lukeson could not help thinking that maybe, if Mellor was in trouble, the kind of trouble that would ruin both their lives, Sarah Mellor might be willing to help him. In his experience, often in times of crisis, former partners at loggerheads united against a common enemy.

And Sarah Mellor had that all important link to the mental hospital . . .

'Will I be charged?' Mellor asked.

'Yes,' Lukeson confirmed bluntly. 'Forensics will need to look the vehicle over.'

When forensics collected the station wagon, Andy Lukeson decided to take some badly needed exercise. Returning a half-hour later, Frank Mellor drove past him.

'Wonder where he's off to,' Lukeson murmured.

★ ★ ★

The young woman who opened the front door looked curiously at the man on her doorstep.

'Sorry to trouble you,' Fred apologized. 'I wonder if you could help me with this address. It's an elderly woman, and I'm worried about her.'

'Of course,' said the young woman, her apprehension gone on seeing who her caller was.

Fred screwed up his eyes in the dusk, to supposedly read the address he had written on the piece of blank paper. 'You need the eyes of an owl,' he joked.

'Please, step into the hall,' the young woman invited.

'Shouldn't you ask your parents first? Or whoever you're living with if that's all right? These are troubled times.'

'No one to ask. I'm home alone.'

Bingo!

'Thanks. You're very kind.' Fred stepped into the hall, and purposely knocked against the hall door to partially close it. 'That's better.' He read from the blank paper. 'Dewsbury Road.' Which he knew was two streets away from where he was. 'Number ten.'

The girl looked puzzled.

'There's no old lady living there,' she said. 'That's my friend Rachel's house.'

Fred thought, how unlucky can one get.

As all murder victims must, in the second before they're attacked, she saw the intent in his eyes. She tried to scream, but the knife in her throat changed her scream to a gurgle, followed by a whimper. Before her eyes dimmed in death, she thought what lovely soft hands you have . . .

So white.

Fred put the dead woman in the passenger seat of the ancient Fiesta he had stolen. He propped her up with a cushion from the driver's seat, and tied a piece of string, which he had blackened with chimney soot to make it invisible, around her forehead and attached it to the headrest to keep her head upright. Then he secured the seatbelt. 'Wouldn't want to be done for not wearing a seatbelt, would you?' Slumped, she would draw attention, and the drive to where he had decided to dump Sally Speckle's next present was at the other side of Loston and many traffic lights away. There was a hell of a risk involved, stopped at junctions as he would be, but it was a risk worth taking. He had dressed her, after undressing her, in a black polo neck to hide the gaping gash in her throat where he had plunged the knife. 'You look the picture of health, my darling,' he said. Driving away, he felt quite chuffed that his boldness had paid off. After being deprived earlier of the woman in the park, he had been frustrated and angry. But now he felt relaxed. He had got his present for Sally Speckle. He was about to pull out when, in the left-hand mirror he spotted a squad car turning into the street at the far end at prowling pace. He let the Fiesta slip back into the parking space, hoping that the police car would take no interest in him. However, as the car got closer it seemed to be moving slower and slower, as if looking for somewhere. His immediate thought was that someone had seen something and had phoned the police. Drawing near, the squaddie slowed to a crawl. He had to do something. Just sitting there made him look suspicious, and the police would almost certainly check him out.

He leaned over and kissed the dead woman.

On the periphery of his vision, Fred could see the driver of the squaddie grinning. He said something to his partner who laughed. They drove on. Fred lay back in the driver's seat, sweat sticking his shirt to his back. He pushed the young woman's tongue which was lolling out of the side of her mouth back in. 'Don't like French, darling,' he said. He put the car in gear, pulled out and drove away.

★ ★ ★

DI Sally Speckle rubbed tired eyes and switched off the desk lamp. She arched her back to try to relax her neck and shoulder muscles, but nothing would work except a hot bath, a stiff drink and to sit in her favourite armchair.

Walking along the short empty corridor leading from her office to the briefing room, she thought that late at night when the hustle and bustle of police work was mostly confined to the custody area, the inner police station was like a deserted planet with only the odd inhabitant wandering about, catching up with what had not been possible to do during the normal working day. It was a time when Sally Speckle always wondered if she had chosen the right career. It was at times like this that she had the feeling that she

145

should be somewhere else, with a working life that was not strewn with dead bodies and constant angst of one kind or another, even on what would be termed a routine day, of which there were fewer and fewer as society became ever more ready to indulge in violence rather than negotiation to solve its differences.

She thought, will I end up like Alice Mulgrave? With only the job and nothing more? Her problem was that she was not sure what she wanted anymore. Like Mulgrave, she suspected that she liked the independence of being unencumbered, and the freedom of being unattached.

She turned left at the end of the hall to make her way past the canteen and out by a side door to the car-park. It was the longer way round, but she just did not have the stomach to go through Custody with its drunks, prostitutes and yobbos.

One of the car-park lights was blown, causing an eerie imbalance of light between intensely bright areas interspersed with darker patches. The overall effect gave the car-park the look of a film set in a slasher movie. Walking through the bright areas Sally Speckle felt exposed, like a stripper in a spotlight, she thought fancifully. While in the darker stretches, she felt threatened and

146

vulnerable. She never had before when one of the lights was on the blink, a not infrequent occurrence. 'You're letting that bastard Fred get to you,' she told herself. She was glad when she reached the Punto, and instantly unhappy on turning the ignition, hearing nothing but the depressing click of a dead battery.

On her third attempt the click had vanished, leaving only empty silence. She slapped her hand on the steering wheel and promised, not for the first time, 'That's it. You're for the knacker's yard!' She could look under the bonnet, but what would be the point? She knew nothing about cars other than how to start them, put them in gear, let out the clutch, move off and steer. Which meant she was stranded. She would have to go back inside and try to arrange a lift home in a squaddie. Or . . . She checked the time — 11.15 p.m. Not too late. She'd phone Andy Lukeson. Ask him to come and collect her. The battery of her mobile was low (a night for low batteries, she thought), so she got out of the car to make the call, hoping that being outside would improve the transmission enough to allow her to contact Andy. She was waiting for Lukeson to answer when she got the most awful urge to spin around, sensing someone watching her. But that was silly, the car-park was secure. A stranger would not encroach any great distance before being apprehended. And yet she could not shake the feeling of eyes on her.

'Lukeson.'

'Andy,' Speckle said gratefully. 'The Punto's on the blink. Can you come and get me, please?'

'Ten minutes,' he said immediately.

'I'm in the car-park.'

'It's turned chilly. Go back inside. I'll collect you from there.'

'You're a brick, Andy,' she said, relieved.

'Is that with a B, I hope so?'

'What? Oh.' She laughed. 'Yes. With a B, Andy.'

DI Sally Speckle tried to make her return to the station leisurely, but she had not got very far before her pace picked up and, by the time she had covered the short distance to the side door through which she had emerged, she was like an Olympic sprinter in training. On getting inside, she stood, back to the wall breathing hard. Relaxing, she made her way to meet Andy at the front of the station.

★ ★ ★

On the drive home, Lukeson brought his DI up to speed on his interview with Frank Mellor. Speckle yawned. 'It's always nice to

148

be appreciated,' Lukeson said, but in a bantering tone.

'Sorry, Andy. Mind if we wait until tomorrow to sift through the possibilities?'

'Will you be OK?' he asked, when they reached Speckle's house. 'Want me to see you inside?'

'I'm a big girl, Andy,' she replied, trying to pass off his offer diplomatically, but managing only to sound stilted and ungrateful.

'See you tomorrow then.'

'Thanks for the lift.'

'What are sergeants for?'

She looked after the departing Lukeson, thinking that the least she could have done was ask him in for a cup of coffee, but she wanted to avoid any awkwardness that might come up. Her problem was that she was not at all sure which of them might have caused that awkwardness, because she was already regretting her hasty dismissal of Andy Lukeson's offer.

Letting herself into the house, jaded, she dropped everything in the hall and turned into the sitting-room to seek the comfort of her favourite armchair only to find that it was already occupied with the dead body of a young woman. A red rose lay on her lap. She knew what the card sellotaped to her forehead would read: *Fred. Kisses.*

11

DI Sally Speckle regained consciousness slowly, as if floating up through a grey world or ascending from a deep sea dive. She floated weightlessly upwards until suddenly, without warning, the light pierced her eyes with ferocious intensity as they shot open and all the horror of the previous night rushed back into her mind with the speed of an express train, vivid in its gruesome detail.

She screamed.

Andy Lukeson rushed into the room. 'Easy,' he said, squeezing her hands in his. 'You're perfectly safe, Sally. A nice sweet cuppa, I think.'

Lying back, she took in her surroundings and wondered why Andy Lukeson lived in such a cramped and poorly kept flat. She had chosen 'poorly kept' as a description, rather that the more appropriate 'grungy'. The carpet had been old when Noah sailed in the Ark, and the black damp patch in the far corner of the room, highlighted even more depressingly by the bright sunshine flooding through the window, hinted at bigger problems to come in the not too distant future. She had a vague recollection from the night before that the remainder of the flat was no better.

Andy arrived back with a steaming cup of tea and toast. 'Get that inside you. It'll make you feel perkier. Doyle phoned. Said to tell you that Mulgrave has asked for a meeting. Phone him back to arrange a suitable time.'

'How about New Year's Eve 2020,' she sighed.

★ ★ ★

'Our Mr Thomas will be with you shortly, Inspector,' Kate, the receptionist at Loston Mental Hospital informed Speckle in response to her request to speak to the hospital administrator. She picked up the tabloid on the desk which she had been glancing through when the DI and Helen Rochester had entered. The screaming headline read:

WOMAN'S BATTERED BODY FOUND IN
FORMER PUB
POLICE HUNT EVIL KILLER

Helen Rochester had already brought the report to Speckle's notice, scripted luridly, every stop pulled out to shock and titillate.

'Terrible, isn't it?' Kate said, inviting comment, but not getting any. Then, her eyes lit up. 'The murder isn't connected with the

151

phone call from here, is it?' Thankfully, Speckle was saved from having to reply when, looking beyond her, the receptionist called out, 'Oh, Mr Shooter. Music-therapy is in Room Ten this morning.'

Speckle turned round.

'Good morning, Mr Shooter. We meet again.'

'You'll forgive me if I tell you that it is *not* a pleasure, Inspector. Why Room Ten?' he quizzed Kate.

'Maintenance found dry rot in part of the floor of Room Six, Mr Shooter. They declared it unsafe for use.'

'I hate change,' Shooter grumbled.

'His hates would be long and many, I reckon,' Rochester said to Speckle, in a whispered aside.

'And will you please inform Mr Thomas' — Shooter's eyes locked with Speckle's — 'that I have a crow to pluck with him.'

'Mr Thomas will be here shortly to see the inspector,' Kate said.

'I'm a very busy man,' Shooter barked. 'Tell him to make himself available after music-therapy.' He swung about on Speckle. 'Now that our paths have unfortunately crossed again, Inspector, I might as well save myself a phone call. Thinking back, something came to mind about the man using the payphone.'

'The man had pale hands. Soft. Like the hands of someone who might wear surgical or rubber gloves a great deal.'

'Like yours, perhaps?' Rochester piped up.

Shooter's gaze came to rest on Helen Rochester, as if he had just discovered something very unpleasant under a stone he had turned over. 'Very observant, Officer. Yes, I do wear gloves a lot in my developing room. Photography is my hobby. But,' he held up his hands for examination, 'mine are a shade rosier than the hands of the payphone user.'

'Were this man's hands strong, Mr Shooter?' Speckle enquired.

'Well, just let's say, Inspector' — he came closer and put his hand on her arm — 'that you would not want them round your pretty neck.'

Speckle pulled away, a sense of maggots under her skin from Shooter's soft touch.

'Yes,' he said bitchily. 'Strong hands, I would say, Inspector.' He turned and strode towards the door near the payphone which led into the inner hospital. Speckle found it hard to believe that, passing so close to the man on the payphone, that Rupert Shooter had not got a better look at him than he was admitting to.

'Did you notice anything about this man's

demeanour that was familiar, Mr Shooter?' she called after him.

'If I had, I would have told you,' he replied sharply.

'Ever been to the Old Mill?'

His face took on an expression of stark fury, as if she had caused the deepest offence. 'I'm not the pub type, Inspector.' He vanished through the door.

'Pompous twit!' Helen Rochester said.

'He knows of the Old Mill,' Speckle said, 'because I never mentioned that it was a pub.'

As the door Shooter had gone through closed, a twin door on the opposite side of reception opened as if connected by elastic and Thomas came through, glancing impatiently at his watch. 'What's this about, Inspector? I hope it won't take too long. I have a meeting with the finance committee in ten minutes.'

'Mr Thomas, the man who made the phone call from the payphone in reception yesterday morning wore a green dressing-gown.'

'That's quite impossible, Inspector. Patients aren't allowed near reception. It would be much too close to the main entrance. Or, in the event of a patient trying to abscond, which is more common than one might imagine, much too close to the exit.'

'My interest, Mr Thomas, is in how

someone other than a patient might acquire a dressing-gown.'

'Why would they want to?'

'Please bear with me,' Speckle said diplomatically, putting on an air of needing guidance. 'Perhaps if you'd explain the procedure.'

'It's quite simple. The orderlies issue the patients with a dressing-gown prior to their going for treatment. A green gown would mean that the patient was on his way to the hydrotherapy unit, Inspector.'

'The patients would not have the gowns themselves, then?'

'Dear me, no. Besides being very expensive, it would cause no end of confusion, Inspector. They would, of course, have a personal dressing-gown, but not one appropriate to their programme. You see, we have different colours for different treatments and programmes, so should any difficulty arise any member of staff could identify where everyone should be and in what programme they are enrolled.'

'Quite ingenious, Mr Thomas,' Speckle said, by way of flattery to an end.

'My idea actually,' Thomas boasted.

'So, let me get this straight. Just before the patients go to a particular programme, the orderlies issue the gowns, correct?'

'Yes.'

'And once these gowns are issued, the patients are escorted immediately to wherever they should be?'

'Yes.'

'Escorted all the way?'

'Of course, Inspector.'

'No staff shortages, then?'

'Well ... nowadays ... tight budgets.' Thomas hunched his shoulders. 'I'm sure the police are no different.'

'Indeed. And yesterday morning's hydrotherapy session. Enough orderlies, were there?'

'There was no danger to patient welfare,' said Thomas defensively.

Feeling there was something that Thomas was holding back, Speckle pressed, 'So yesterday morning, everything went smoothly with the hydrotherapy session?'

Thomas's shoulders slumped.

'One of the patients threw a tantrum, I'm afraid, became quite disruptive, with an unfortunate knock-on effect on his fellow patients.'

'Sounds rather difficult,' Speckle said.

'Disastrous would be a more precise description, Inspector,' said Thomas, glumly.

'So it's possible that during this confused and difficult period, a dressing-gown might

156

have gone missing briefly?'

Shocked, Thomas asked, 'You mean someone, unauthorized, might have taken it? Certainly not, Inspector.'

'How can you be so sure? It would seem that the situation was quite chaotic.'

'Well, of course, I can't be absolutely sure, but all the dressing-gowns were accounted for when the patient was subdued and the disturbance was brought under control.'

'What started it, Mr Thomas?'

'It's all a tad unclear. It seems that the patient, who has an extraordinary devotion to his wife, was told that she was out . . . well . . . whoring, was the term used, I believe.'

'Who told the patient this?'

'I don't know.'

'Can't the patient recall?'

'These are deeply disturbed individuals, Inspector, experiencing only flashes of rationality and lucidity. The patient in question has incipient dementia.'

Clearly, whoever it was who wanted to get their hands on a dressing-gown has an intimate knowledge of what would most upset this patient, Speckle thought. And even if the patient had remembered who it was, with the onset of dementia, it would be easy to fob off his accusation.

'It was all rather unfortunate,' Thomas

said, 'and with the Board of Trustees present. Mr Ambrose, the chairman of the board, even though in his seventies, takes a special interest in innovative programmes like hydrotherapy.'

'How long did this disturbance last, Mr Thomas?'

'Longer than it should have. All told, it took about fifteen minutes to restore calm fully. We were fortunate to have some staff from Loston General Hospital along at the time to help out. From time to time patients have to attend at the general hospital, and staff come to collect them. A couple attend regularly. Kidney problems. Diabetes, that kind of thing.' Mr Thomas checked his watch worriedly. 'I really should be getting along.'

'What grades of staff, Mr Thomas?' Speckle asked.

'Nursing staff from the department involved. Of course, they would be accompanied by a porter or two. Some of the patients can become quite difficult. Now I really . . . ' Thomas waved to some unseen destination behind the door through which he had appeared.

'One more thing, Mr Thomas. My colleague and I would like to talk to the patients and staff who were at the hydrotherapy session in question.'

'The orderlies won't be a problem, but interviewing Loston General Staff is a matter

158

for them. And the patients, well that's out of my hands, Inspector,' Thomas said, relieved. 'Such a request would come under what's best for a patient, and would have to be decided by Professor Stanley, our Medical Director.'

'I'm sure it would help if you had a word, Mr Thomas,' the DI said diplomatically. 'Smooth the way, so to speak.'

Thomas seemed to grow in stature. 'Well, it might, I suppose.'

'Would you, please?'

'If I can help, of course, Inspector.'

'Thank you.'

'If you'll follow me. Stanley's office is on the way to the finance committee meeting.'

'Did you notice anyone leave the hydrotherapy session during the disturbance you spoke of?' Speckle questioned, as they walked along a dark hallway, fit, Helen Rochester thought, to give anyone the willies.

'No. But then with all the confusion, and the safety of the trustees to consider . . . You understand, Inspector.'

'Of course.'

'Perhaps, someone who shouldn't be there, then?'

'I can't see any reason why someone who should not have been there, would have been there, Inspector.'

She could. Someone who wanted to get their hands on a dressing-gown. The iniquitous Fred, for example.

'When the dressing-gowns are issued, is there any overlap?' Rochester enquired. 'For example, if staff were hard pressed, might the gowns be issued some time before to the patients? Or perhaps there might be a delay in collecting them after the session?'

'Most unlikely,' Thomas said.

'But it could happen?' Rochester pressed.

'I suppose anything can happen, Sergeant,' Thomas said coolly.

Thomas came to a door outside which a woman was standing, all a dither. From inside the office, came the sounds of a disturbance.

'What on earth is going on, Ms Jones?' Thomas enquired, concerned. He glanced in astonishment at the door bearing the brass name plate announcing: MEDICAL DIRECTOR, when a bass voice called out from inside, 'You little bastard!'

'Mice,' Ms Jones explained to an astonished Thomas. 'At least one. Professor Stanley is trying to catch it. Ran across the floor near my desk.' She shivered, hand on heart. 'I nearly fainted.'

'Oh, dear me,' Thomas grumbled. 'I do hope we haven't an infestation. One ran

160

across my desk only yesterday. Brite, one of our contract cleaners,' he explained to Speckle and Rochester, 'dealt with it while I went off to meet the trustees at the hydrotherapy unit.'

DI Sally Speckle reacted. 'You left Brite alone? But you told me that he was in your office at the time I enquired about, Mr Thomas.'

'He was.'

'Yes, but I assumed that you were with him. But if you weren't . . . ' Speckle looked along the hall which led to reception, less than a minute away. 'How far from here is the hydrotherapy unit?'

Thomas pointed to double doors a short distance along the hall. 'Through there. The unit is at the end of a short hall.'

'Did Brite come to the unit to give you the all-clear, Mr Thomas?'

'Yes.'

'During the disturbance?'

'No, Inspector. At that point the disturbance had not begun. But it did moments later. In fact Brite was right on my heels. Nabbed the mouse with admirable speed, actually.'

Brite had the time and the opportunity Sally remarked to herself. He was within easy reach of the payphone. He was also within

161

easy reach of the hydrotherapy unit which went into an uproar shortly after he arrived there, making his task of getting his hands on a patient's dressing-gown all the easier. And he had a legitimate reason to be there, to give Thomas the all-clear, so that would make him part of the scene and he would not come under scrutiny. In his line of work, Brite would also wear rubber gloves daily which would give him pale hands. And he had a history of making nasty phone calls to women. But would he have been privy to the kind of information needed to get the patient so worked up? Being around the hospital every day, a cleaner would have general access, so it was not beyond the bounds of possibility.

'Did Brite speak to the patient who became upset, Mr Thomas?'

'I was rather busy with the trustees, Inspector.'

'Did Mr Brite help to restore order, Mr Thomas?' Speckle enquired.

'I can't recall that he did, actually, Inspector.'

'Was he there at the end of the disturbance?'

Thomas focused his mind.

'Yes,' he stated quite positively. 'I believe he was. Is that in some way important, Inspector?'

'Oh, just fixing the general picture in my

mind, Mr Thomas,' Speckle said.

It was clear that Fred's whispering in a patient's ear about his wife's disloyalty was part and parcel of his overall plan to cause a scene, the purpose of which was to get his hands on a patient's dressing-gown and return it during the confusion when everyone else's attention would be diverted. Without the disturbance, an important part of Fred's plan would have failed.

The sequence of events had to be:

CCTV down. Opportunity presented.

Murder.

Disturbance.

Dressing-gown.

Phone call.

'Do you know if Brite is friendly with this patient, Mr Thomas?'

'I can't imagine how he would be, but, of course, Brite has been around for quite some time. And on the odd occasion, very odd,' he stressed, 'a patient might prevail upon someone like Brite to do a simple errand for them. Or fetch something they needed.'

Thomas was on the defensive again.

'As you can well understand, I'm sure, Inspector. Like police officers, not being able to be on every street corner, it's not possible either to have an orderly at the end of every bed.'

163

'Of course not, Mr Thomas,' Speckle sympathized. 'So a bond of sorts might develop between a patient and a regular person about the hospital.'

'Bond, you say,' Thomas said uncomfortably. 'That would be putting it a bit strongly, Inspector.'

So Brite might indeed have been privy to what would disturb the patient, had he gained his confidence. Distressed people often spoke of their inner feelings to complete strangers, and even more so to someone with whom they became friendly, but not a friend as such. Had that happened, Brite might very well have known what buttons to push.

Opportunity and motive had to exist for murder. Brite may very well have had the opportunity, but what could his motive for murdering Claire Shaw have been? Might he have met her in the Old Mill? Might he have suffered the same gut-wrenching rejection Shaw had given others? By its description, the Old Mill might very well have been the kind of establishment that Brite would frequent. His alibi was no more, and he would have known that it was not an alibi at all when she and Lukeson had interviewed him, but he had let them think it was. It was a gamble that might very well have paid off — would have paid off, had a mouse not shattered it.

164

The mouse.

And therein lay the real crux in putting Larry Brite firmly in the frame. He could not have depended on a mouse to conveniently sprint across Thomas's desk.

Unless . . .

'Did you summon Mr Brite to deal with the mouse in your office, Mr Thomas?'

'No. As good fortune would have it, he had dropped by my office to bring my attention to a leaking urinal in a staff toilet.'

A urinal damaged by Brite to give him the excuse to be in Thomas's office to plant the mouse? Sally mused. Was Brite that clever? That good a planner? Was the mouse in Professor Stanley's office the same mouse that was let loose by Brite and never recaptured? He being much too busy trying to get his hands on a patient's dressing-gown.

'I was rather upset at the time,' Thomas intoned haughtily.

'Why was that, Mr Thomas?' Speckle enquired.

'Well, Inspector, damaged staff urinals are a matter for maintenance, not the hospital administrator. And Brite should have known this, but as it turned out, under the circumstances, Brite's ignorance of procedure was my good fortune, Inspector. Of course, I have now put him right on how things should be done in the future.'

'How long has Mr Brite been working at the hospital, Mr Thomas?'

'I couldn't be certain offhand, Inspector; he seems to have been around for an age.'

DI Sally Speckle thought, long enough to know that the hospital administrator should not have been bothered with a report about a damaged urinal. So, Brite had gone to Thomas's office with a mouse in his pocket — being a cleaner he'd know where to catch one — Thomas gained him admittance to the hydrotherapy unit and it was there that he had got his hands on a dressing-gown?

'Did you ask Mr Brite to report to you at the hydrotherapy unit, Mr Thomas?' Speckle asked.

'No. I was rather annoyed when he did, actually, Inspector, but I suppose he did it out of the best of intentions.'

DI Sally Speckle was of a mind to doubt that very much.

12

DC Charlie Johnson climbed the rickety stairs of 13 Archer Street, which had been once an elegant family home, but was now at the end of a long line of landlords whose lack of dedication to even the minimum degree of maintenance, let alone restoration, was evident in every inch of the building.

The smell of curry predominated.

'Mr Frederics?' Johnson enquired of the man who answered his knock.

'Never heard of no Frederics,' said the man in a surly voice.

'And you are?'

'Who's doin' the askin'?' Johnson showed his warrant card. 'Ryan's the name.'

'Somehow, I don't believe you, Mr Ryan,' Johnson said.

'That's me name,' he said grumpily.

'About having never heard of Benny Frederics,' Johnson said.

Ryan shrugged. 'Your choice, ain't it.'

'You have a choice, too,' said Charlie Johnson, grimfaced. 'You can tell me where I'll find Frederics and I'll leave, as if I've never been here, or I'll make your life as miserable as I possibly can, and that, Mr Ryan, will be very miserable indeed.'

It took all of a second for Ryan to come to a decision. '6 Oak Street. The bell slot will have Beth Mullins on it. Frederics is her pimp. Don't tell him I told you. Fred's a crack freak.'

'Fred?' Johnson questioned urgently.

'Yeah, Fred, Frederics, get it? That's what he likes to be called. Hates being called Benny. Says it's a poofs name. So he calls himself Fred.'

Going downstairs, Johnson's mobile rang. He announced himself, and greeted cordially, 'Mr Lancome . . . ' He listened. 'I see. Well, thank you anyway. She didn't mention who her dentist was? Pity.' Lancome was one of the dentists he had phoned in his search for Claire Shaw's dentist. He recalled Shaw from a couple of weeks before. She had been a casual patient who'd had a filling that had popped out and needed replacing — an emergency patient who would return to her own dentist. So her dental records would be with him.

★   ★   ★

'Police?' queried Professor James Stanley. He was a long string of a man who would have

168

been a perfect fit in an advert for famine relief. He looked out after Mr Thomas as he vanished from the Medical Director's office, throwing back introductions behind him. Stanley had a surprisingly mellifluous voice, which was quite unexpected emanating from such a spare frame.

'Did you catch the mouse, Professor?' Ms Jones asked, looking nervously about the cluttered office which offered a thousand places for a mouse to hide.

'Fraid not, Melanie. Last sighting was over there.'

He pointed to a corner which was home to a stack of old files gathering dust. Clearly Stanley was a hoarder.

'Oh, no,' Melanie Jones squealed, in a fashion that might just attract the mouse out, thinking it had heard a mating call.

'A brave heart, Melanie,' Stanley said. 'It'll make a mistake. They always do. And then,' Stanley slapped his hands together to indicate the mouse's annihilation. He turned to Speckle. 'Now, as I was saying, I'm not sure — '

'It's to do with the patients in the hydrotherapy programme, Professor,' Speckle explained.

'Oh, that,' he intoned tiredly. Obviously Stanley was not an advocate of hydrotherapy.

169

'Nowadays there are all sorts of programmes and therapies.' That statement put him firmly in the traditionalist camp. 'Music-therapy. Hydrotherapy. A mishmash of Eastern nonsense and' — he cast his eyes upwards — 'heaven forbid, Californian whackery.'

He went on apace.

'In my opinion, Inspector,' which Speckle guessed was freely and regularly given. 'The mentally ill can be done more harm than good by ill-advised treatments which seem to work for film and pop stars, but have very little value to the ordinary man and woman who become afflicted. False hope in this business is damaging.'

He looked with steely grey eyes at Speckle.

'Police officers traipsing about the place don't help either. Seeing that their incarceration here involved, in many cases, legal proceedings of one kind or another, a lot of patients in here are either very mistrustful of the police or resent them.'

'It's imperative that I speak to the patients who were engaged in hydrotherapy yesterday morning at around nine thirty, Professor,' Speckle stated.

'What's imperative to you doesn't really matter,' Stanley said, stiffly. 'I'll be the arbiter of what is good for the patients of this hospital. An explanation of the absolute

170

necessity of your request might be constructive, Inspector.'

She gave it in one word. 'Murder.'

Taken aback, Stanley asked, 'Whose murder?'

'Have you read today's papers?'

'You mean the woman found in the former Old Mill pub?'

'Yes.'

'Miss it,' Stanley sighed. 'Had great atmosphere. Like one of those seedy bars in the Far East. The kind of place where skullduggery was never far away in the murky smokiness. Now sadly, in the main, these havens of mystery and intrigue and no small risk of food poisoning, have been replaced by establishments' — his face took on the desolation of despair — 'that are smoke free, lager drenched, flashing lights, laptop dancers and yobbo tourist havens, inhabited by people who want to spend their budget holidays in the same kind of grotty establishments they left behind. Why bother, I say. I mean, could the most imaginative among us see Humphrey Bogart or Claude Rains strolling nonchalantly into one of these places?'

He glanced from Speckle to Rochester.

'You do know who Bogart and Rains were, don't you?'

Bogart they could both acknowledge, but Rains was someone, to Stanley's horror, that they could not place.

'*Casablanca,*' he wailed, and encouraged, 'The police officer: Captain Louis Renault.'

'Oh, yes,' Rochester said, not wanting to send Stanley into deep despair.

'You frequented the Old Mill, Professor?' Speckle asked, returning to the business on hand, a touch surprised that a man of the professor's eminence should be a customer of Archie Tattan's dive.

'Oh, yes,' Stanley told Speckle. 'The Old Mill had a certain romance about it, Inspector.'

'Romance?' DC Helen Rochester intoned, astonished.

'Yes. It had an air of the unexpected about it, and that surely is the very essence of romance? I have a secret to confess to,' Stanley said, in a hushed tone. Speckle and Rochester exchanged expectant glances. 'I'm a bit of a scribe: short stories. Nothing good enough to make it to print, yet, but the Old Mill was chockful of characters and scenes more alive and vibrant than any writer could create. All I had to do was simply lift them from life and put them in my stories.'

He scratched his grey head.

'It's getting the scenes to come alive on paper with the same verve that's the problem.'

'You must have known the people there,

172

then?' Rochester said.

'Oh, not personally, no. There was one, a chap called Benny Frederics, got him a porter's job here at the hospital. Wish I hadn't.'

'Did you perhaps know a woman by the name of Claire Shaw, Pofessor?' Speckle questioned.

'No, Inspector. Is that the name of the woman who was murdered?'

'I'm sorry, as yet, we can't confirm any details.'

'What's her murder got to do with wanting to interview the patients in hydrotherapy, Inspector? Locked in here, none of those patients could have murdered her.'

Sally Speckle explained the significance of her request.

'So you think that this chap who phoned you from the payphone in reception works at the hospital and stole this dressing-gown to disguise that fact?'

'I believe so, Professor. And that's why we need to speak to the patients. To ascertain if anyone saw — '

'Waste of time,' Stanley interjected. 'Lucidity and rationality with these patients is about as rare as snow in July.'

'With climate change, who knows,' Rochester quipped.

Stanley cast an eye on Rochester that would have put wrinkles on a potato.

'Police work is a lot like psychiatry, Professor,' Speckle said. 'Sometimes, out of the blue, comes a glimmer of understanding that makes sense of the previously impenetrable.'

Fortunately for Helen Rochester, Stanley removed his gaze from her before she turned from wrinkled potato to dried prune.

'Knowing these patients, that to me, Inspector, sounds like wishful thinking. But far be it from me to crush hope. There were four patients.' His long, tapering fingers flashed across a computer keyboard on his desk, Speckle thought that he would probably have made a wonderful concert pianist, such was his manual dexterity. 'All male.' He sprang out of his chair, and was at the door of the office in a couple of loping strides. 'Follow me, ladies.'

'About the mouse, Professor,' Melanie Jones asked, her eyes flashing about.

'Go to the canteen. Get a bit of cheese. Put it on the floor over there.' He pointed to the cluttered corner. 'When it comes out. Step on it good and hard.'

Melanie Jones might have woken with Dracula at her throat. Stanley paused in the open door.

'On second thoughts,' he said. 'Get someone to deal with it. I doubt very much if even a starving mouse would eat canteen cheese. Come along Inspector,' he called, leading the way along the hall with strides that a bush kangaroo would have been hard pressed to keep pace with.

★ ★ ★

DC Charlie Johnson arrived at 6 Oak Street, a structure only moderately better than the one he had left five minutes before. He went up the cracked and disintegrating steps and pressed the bell with the name Beth Mullins attached.

'Yeah?' came the bored response over the intercom.

'Ms Mullins?' Johnson enquired.

'I ain't doin' no business today, love,' she said. The intercom went dead. Johnson buzzed again. 'I told you — '

'Police.'

'Flat four,' said Beth Mullins resignedly.

He climbed a staircase covered with a threadbare carpet whose unruly patches and ragged edges would sooner or later cause someone to tumble, if it had not already done so. He passed a loo that would make a war-zone latrine look respectable. Flat 4 was easily identified by the woman in its open door, who was dressed to titilate. Beth Mullins might not have been doing business, but she was most certainly in character.

'Haven't seen you before,' she said, turning back into the flat. 'You'll have to be quick. My boyfriend is due back any time now, and there'll be trouble if he finds you here.'

'I think there's been a misunderstanding,' Johnson said, following her into the flat.

'I doubt it,' she said. 'You're a copper, lookin' for a freebie. So how would you like it to be delivered? Got to pay my dues for a quiet life, don't I?'

'I'm here to talk to Benny Frederics, Ms Mullins,' Johnson said stiffly.

'Fred? Oh, that's what he likes to be called. He thinks Benny sounds poncy. Me, I prefer Benny. He's not here.'

'Where might I find him?'

'No idea. He's been in one of his moods this last coupla weeks. Takes off. Might see him in an hour, a day, a week, who knows. I keep tellin' him to quit drugs, but he don't listen. To be honest with ya, I'd prefer it if he fell down a mineshaft and was never seen again, but don't tell him that. Might end up in a trunk in a railway station cloakroom.'

She frowned.

'Do railway stations still have cloakrooms?

Such a bloody waste, too. Benny could've been anythin' he wanted to be, I reckon.'

'Violent when he's strung out, is he?'

'Let's just say that he's best left alone then.'

'Why do you stay around?'

'Well, I thought about movin' to my country estate,' said Beth Mullins sarcastically. 'But,' she waved her hand over the gloomy, damp, grungy flat that had a pair of cockroaches fighting over a crumb on the table, 'why would I want to leave all this, eh? Now,' she smiled, in a way she was used to smiling when hooking a punter, 'do you want that freebie or not?'

★ ★ ★

The phone on WPC Anne Fenning's desk rang. 'Father Lake,' she greeted her caller. 'Good to hear from you so soon.' Her compliment was a genuine one. The clergyman who had been assigned the task of checking church records for Jack Ansome's name was a very pleasant man. She listened. 'I see. That is interesting. Thank you for getting back to us so promptly, Father. Goodbye.'

'Well now, Jack Ansome was never a priest,' she told PC Brian Scuttle, who was just returning from an unfruitful visit to Loston's

177

gyms, looking for a man who might have been in training but who had packed it in.

The overall vague description of the man Shooter had seen on the payphone was pretty useless and made no impression.

'Needle in a haystack, ain't it?' his second last gym manager had said, which for Scuttle about summed it up.

'In these security-conscious days, don't you have photo ID of your customers?' Scuttle had asked. Most had not, and those who had only kept it on file for a brief period after the customer quit.

'Ansome had a short stay in a seminary, but got kicked out, Brian,' Fenning reported. 'The church authorities put out the word, and no one would touch our Jack after that. Psychologically unsuitable for Holy Orders, was the verdict. Apparently Ansome had a morbid interest in the dead, particularly the female dead.'

'A cleaning lady found a stash of photographs of nude women hidden in his room, their bits and pieces gaudily obliterated with a felt pen. The back of the pictures had disturbing sexual references, and how these harlots, Father Lake's words, should be punished; a punishment that could be death. The cleaner was quite shocked and brought the photographs to the attention of Ansome's

178

superior, who gave our Jack the heave-ho. After that all doors were closed to him.'

'Did the church report this to the police?' Scuttle asked.

'Apparently not.'

'A potential nutter, and they did nothing?'

'They like to keep things in-house, Brian.'

'That was bloody stupid. Looks like we might have found our killer, eh?'

13

Two orderlies ushered the four patients into the bare and depressing room, unfurnished except for four plastic chairs — 'Enough to drive anyone bonkers,' DC Helen Rochester said, in an aside to Sally Speckle. Speckle saw little hope of learning anything from the shuffling, sad-faced men.

'I warned you, Inspector, that it would be a pretty useless exercise,' Stanley reminded her, on seeing her disappointment.

The orderlies sat the patients down, stepped back, but not too far away, ready to restrain the men should it become neccessary. Professor Stanley introduced Speckle and Rochester, not that it seemed to make any difference to the men. Speckle looked at the name tags the men wore:

James.

Larry.

Jack.

Simon.

'Which man caused the disturbance in the hydrotherapy unit?' Speckle asked Stanley quietly.

'Jack.'

Looking at the pathetic crouched figure, Speckle could not imagine him animated enough to throw the most minor of tantrums.

'Hello,' she said. Sad, empty eyes, like curtainless windows, looked back at her. She wished she had greater experience in dealing with mentally ill people and did not feel as out of her depth as she did. She had only once before had to question a mentally ill person and, unfortunately, they had to be sectioned. 'My name is Detective Inspector Sally Speckle, and I want to ask you some questions. All right with you?'

'I like being asked questions,' Larry said. 'Sometimes when I'm asked questions, the voices in my head stop talking to me. It's so peaceful then. All that chatter can be so annoying.'

'Mary?' The man called Simon jumped up. 'Is that you?'

The orderlies moved towards the man, but Speckle waved them away. 'No, Simon. I'm not Mary. My name is Sally.'

'Don't know any Sally,' Simon said, sadly. Then he brightened. 'If you see Mary, will you tell her I still love her?'

'Of course I will.'

Simon sat back down and bent over to put his head between his legs, rocking back and forth, mumbling. Speckle was overwhelmed by the enormity of her task, and was about to suggest another time to Stanley, if there ever could be a right time, when suddenly James said with absolute clarity, 'What is it you want to know, Inspector?'

'Well, do you recall your hydrotherapy session yesterday morning, James?'

'Yes. How could I forget it?' He cast a malevolent glare at Jack. 'Got into a right strop, did Jack.' He was well spoken. His voice had a military clip to it. He had been, Speckle reckoned, a man used to giving orders.

'You wear a special dressing-gown going to hydrotherapy . . . '

'Is that what they call that rag?' James snorted. 'Any self-respecting dog wouldn't lie on one.'

'Are you sure you're not Mary?' Simon asked.

'Yes, Simon,' Speckle said, annoyed at the interruption which might lose her James's moment of clarity.

Simon giggled. 'Oh, dear. Silly me. Mary's dead. I killed her.' Simon's laughter became manic. 'Hit her with a car-jack. Don't know what all the fuss was about,' he said puzzled. 'I just wanted to see what was inside her silly head.'

'Whore!' Jack raged and sprang out of the chair.

The orderlies were upon him in seconds to restrain him, and sit him firmly back down, remaining close at hand. Speckle reckoned that Jack had referred to his wife, and thought it might be an opportune moment to raise what had happened in the hydrotherapy unit, and who might have told him that his wife was whoring.

Shrewdly reading her thoughts, Stanley dismissed the idea with a firm shake of his head.

'Stay put, you idiot,' James barked, his reprimand instantly taking the fight out of Jack who, with a long weary sigh slipped back into docility. The others, too, looked with trepidation at James. Obviously, he was the dominant force within the group.

With Jack subdued and sulking, Speckle concentrated on James. Rochester was of a mind to take James to task, but fortunately recognized before she spoke that her knowledge of how to handle the mentally disturbed could be put through the eye of a needle and still leave room for the camel and a rich man to pass through.

Assuming her impression of James as being of a military background was correct and therefore that he was someone who would appreciate a no-nonsense approach, Speckle came straight to the point, hoping that she was on the right track.

'James, during the disturbance yesterday at the hydrotherapy unit, a dressing-gown was borrowed by someone. Did you see who that person was?'

He became instantly wary, his gaze flicking between Stanley and the orderlies, lingering just a fraction longer on the Medical Director. He leaned towards Speckle, urging her to come to meet him. Stanley beckoned to one of the orderlies, who moved quickly between James and Speckle.

'We must be careful, Inspector,' Stanley said.

'I feel perfectly safe, Professor.'

'Can't take any risks. Sorry.'

'I didn't think she'd have as much mush inside her head,' Simon said vaguely. 'Looked like pink cabbage. And I detest cabbage.'

'Who took the dressing-gown, James?' Speckle asked.

'Inspector, I think it would be wise to end this here and now,' Stanley said.

Looking hunted, James said with an exaggerated yawn, 'Tired. Want to leave now.'

'Enough!' the Medical Director ordered, when Speckle attempted to continue.

'Were you the orderlies on duty yesterday morning?' Speckle asked.

'It was my day off,' said the orderly, who

had not intervened.

'So, who was your replacement?'

'There wasn't one,' Stanley said. 'A nurse from Loston General Hospital who was to escort Simon to dialysis helped out, along with a porter with him. Some of the patients need to attend the general hospital.'

'I know. Mr Thomas told us.'

'Latrine,' James suddenly said, confirming his military background.

'Someone took your dressing-gown while you were at the toilet?' Speckle asked.

'Look,' said the orderly restraining James. 'They get all sorts of notions. James has long conversations with Adolf Hitler, telling him how he cocked up the winter campaign in Russia. You can see what Simon's like. And the others have their moments, too.'

'Whore!' Jack screamed, and sprang out of his chair again, this time necessitating the intervention of both orderlies who had to struggle to restrain him.

The sudden potential for violence triggered a response in the others, and a terrible ugliness was suddenly in the room. Speckle and Rochester felt like humans, helpless and trapped by wild animals.

'Out this way, Inspector,' Stanley said, hurrying Speckle and Rochester to a concealed door in the wall behind them. He

185

activated an alarm on the wall as he went. They found themselves in a small, dark, airless room. He ushered them quickly out of the room into a hallway. 'That was bloody stupid,' he berated Speckle. 'You might want answers, but you'll not get them at the expense of my patients' well-being. Is that fully understood?'

Not willing to be cowed, Speckle enquired, 'When can I see James again, Professor?'

'Again?' he barked, and strode off.

'James could know the name of a killer, Professor,' she called after him, and added, 'A killer who might be just beginning a spree.'

DC Helen Rochester flashed her superior a surprised glance. DI Sally Speckle was a cautious officer, not given to shock tactics.

'It's the only bloody way, Helen,' Speckle said, understanding the import of her DC's look.

Stanley paused and turned. 'A serial killer, Inspector?'

'I think so, Professor.'

'A settling down period will be required,' he said.

'How long a period?'

'I really can't say,' Stanley said. 'An assessment will have to be made of today's episode. The best I can do is to let you know, Inspector. And that will have to satisfy you.'

He turned and walked away.

'Another bloody second and we'd have had a name, Helen.' Speckle thumped her clenched fist on the panelled wall, rocking the painting of a serious, bearded figure of Victorian vintage. And, then with exasperation, 'Just another second, Helen.' Looking down she repeated despondently, 'Just another bloody second!'

14

DC Charlie Johnson was attempting to pull out into the traffic on Oak Street, which was queuing behind a truck that had broken down on a junction, when he saw a man coming along the street looking jittery and continually checking behind him. A van flashed him out, but he ignored the invitation and eased back into the parking space, because he reckoned that he was looking at Benny Frederics who, interestingly, preferred to be called Fred. Going past, the van driver glared. Before getting from his car, Johnson phoned Brigham nick to request back-up. Frederics was a crack user, and could, therefore be unpredictable and possibly dangerous. The time it took to make the phone call worked against Johnson. A woman leaving, let Frederics into the house. He hurried after the woman, warrant card ready to flash.

'I need to get into the house you've just left, urgently, madam. Thanks,' he said a moment later. He closed the door, but left it unlocked to facilitate a quick entry by his Brigham colleagues should such be necessary.

When he reached Mullins' flat, there was a heated argument in progress.

'None of your fucking business where I got to!' Frederics ranted.

'You've been gone hours. It's another woman, ain't it?'

Frederics laughed meanly. 'Yeah, that's right. Another bird. One who's not a slag putting it about for everyone.'

'You bastard. Get out!'

'Get out?' he scoffed. There was the sound of a fist meeting flesh. Beth Mullins cried out. 'I'm not going anywhere, you hear. You hear?' he roared.

'You stay away from me, Benny,' Mullins pleaded.

'Fred's my name. I told you a million times that Benny's a ponce's name. You need to be taught a lesson, you stupid cow,' he said menacingly.

Johnson was about to put his shoulder to the door of the flat when Mullins said, 'The police were lookin' for you.'

'Police?' Instant alarm. 'When?'

Johnson waited.

'Just before you got back. Surprisin' you didn't bump into each other.'

'Shit.' There was sudden fear in Frederics's voice.

'Maybe you weren't as clever as you

189

thought you was when you robbed that old woman over on Sykes Street last week,' Mullins said cockily, positions now reversed. 'If I was you, I'd scarper while I could.'

'Did you tell the filth about the old woman? Because if you did . . . '

'I never tell coppers nothin'. Like I said, you'd better be off before they come back.'

The door of the flat was yanked open and Frederics burst out, straight into DC Charlie Johnson, who grabbed him and pinned him against the wall.

'I'll do you,' Frederics shouted back into the flat.

'I swear I didn't tell 'em nothin',' Beth Mullins wailed.

'She didn't tell me anything, Frederics,' Johnson confirmed.

'Expect me to believe that, do you?' Frederics snarled.

'And, if you take this copper's advice, you'll not bother her again. And now that that's out of the way, I'm arresting you for questioning in connection with . . . '

Expert in the art of escaping from trouble, having served a long apprenticeship, Frederics dropped his free hand and grabbed Johnson by the genitals and squeezed as hard as he could. Johnson fell back. Frederics slipped his hold and leaped over the bannister. He crashed down on to the stairs below, howled, and rolled down the remainder to the hall clutching his right leg. He was hobbling away when the front door crashed in, and two burly constables blocked Frederics's path.

No one was of a mind to show him any sympathy, least of all DC Charlie Johnson, the veins of whose neck and face still bulged as he came gingerly downstairs.

★ ★ ★

'Not you lot again,' Larry Brite groaned. 'I ain't done nothin'.'

'For a start, you gave me a false alibi,' DI Sally Speckle said, her humour grim. 'Thomas left you alone in his office.'

'Are you OK, love?' his wife asked, coming from the kitchen. 'Ain't you never goin' to leave my Larry be?'

'Don't let them fish fingers burn!' he barked. 'Get back in the kitchen.'

'You ungrateful shite,' Mrs Brite yelled.

'Don't make me belt ya one,' Brite said, raising an arm which Rochester grabbed.

'I hope they do ya good and proper this time, Larry Brite,' his wife ranted. 'You lot be sure to throw away the key.' She stormed back into the kitchen.

'About that alibi, Brite,' Speckle said.

'I was scared, wasn't I? You were lookin' for a bloke who made a nasty phone call. I reckoned that wiv my little slip a while back, you'd take the easy option and make the facts fit the bloke.'

Loath though she was to admit it, there had been a few times in the past which lent credence to Brite's claim.

'Ever been to the Old Mill pub?' DC Helen Rochester enquired.

'No.'

'Know where it is?'

'Yeah. But if you're offerin', it ain't no more.'

'Ever heard of a woman called Claire Shaw?'

'No.'

'Sure? We'll find out if you have, Brite,' Speckle promised.

'I told ya. I don't know no Claire Shaw!'

'Enjoy your fish fingers.'

'Fat chance,' he growled.

'And keep your hands off your wife,' Rochester warned.

The front door slammed shut.

'What do you think?' Rochester asked, as they made their way to the Punto, complete with new battery.

'The finger is pointing,' Speckle said in

answer to Rochester's question. 'But, Brite as a killer . . . ?' The DI pulled a face.

'I'd put him right up there,' Rochester said.

Speckle's mobile rang. 'Speckle,' she answered, then mouthed, 'Alison Crewe,' silently to Rochester. 'What? Are you sure? Sorry, of course you are. Thank you for calling.'

Gobsmacked, Speckle broke the connection.

'What?' Rochester asked, intrigued.

'The dead woman's kidneys are perfectly healthy. No sign of disease at all.'

'But that means . . . '

'That the murdered woman is not Claire Shaw, Helen.'

'Bloody Jerusalem,' Helen Rochester exclaimed.

15

'No one home,' Speckle said, stepping back to view the very impressive Gladstone Square house in which Claire Shaw lived. 'I must look out for a rich man. But knowing my luck, I'll end up marrying a DS.' She winced. She had spoken without thinking and it looked, judging by Andy Lukeson's expression, that what had been intended as a witticism had backfired badly.

'Nice to know what rung of the social ladder I'm on,' he responded.

Speckle wished she could say something to assuage his obvious sense of grievance, but nothing she could say right then would have achieved the desired outcome, and would probably only compound an already bad gaffe.

'Can I help you?'

Speckle and Lukeson swung around. The woman who had addressed them had a holdall slung over her shoulder, bearing a sticker of the Eiffel Tower. She was wearing a sleeveless top, and on her arm was displayed the very distinctive tattoo that had so wrongfully formed the basis for the identity of the woman found at the Old Mill.

'Claire Shaw?' Speckle enquired.

'Yes.'

'DI Sally Speckle and DS Andy Lukeson.'

Her concern was immediate. 'What's happened?'

'Perhaps it would be best if we went inside.'

Once inside, Shaw called out, 'Lucy, I'm home.' When no response came, she became alarmed. 'Has something happened to Lucy?'

'Who is Lucy?' Speckle asked.

'Lucy Brett. She's my cousin. She's been housesitting while I was away. Oh, God, something terrible has happened, hasn't it? Tell me what's happened.'

'Do you have a photograph of Ms Brett?' Andy Lukeson asked.

'Somewhere. But looking at me, you're looking at Lucy. We're cousins, but we really are like identical twins. Apparently it's some genetic quirk that pops up every third generation.'

'Down to the tattoo?'

'Yes. Lucy is an even more fanatical Man U supporter than I am. Look, will you please tell me what's happened?'

'We believe that Ms Brett has been murdered, Ms Shaw.'

Andy Lukeson caught Claire Shaw as she staggered backwards. 'Perhaps a drink,' he suggested, leading her into what turned out to be the dining-room.

'Sorry,' Speckle apologized. 'But there's no easy way to break that kind of news.'

'A brandy wouldn't go amiss,' Shaw said, collapsing on to a chair. She pointed to a very cleverly camouflaged drinks cabinet. 'Who'd want to murder, Lucy?' she enquired of Speckle. 'She was the sweetest, most inoffensive person I've ever known.' She held her head in her hands. 'Oh, God, why did I persuade her to housesit for me? There've been several burglaries in the area, you see.' She stared at Speckle. 'Was it a burglary that went wrong?'

'We don't think so,' Speckle said.

Lukeson came back with the brandy and Shaw drank it in one gulp.

'Do you think you could fetch that photograph for us?' Lukeson enquired.

'I think there's a head and shoulders in the desk drawer in the study.' She left, and was back in a short time. 'As you can see, Lucy and I were uncannily alike. Lucy being murdered makes no sense, Inspector.'

Looking at the photograph, Speckle thought: it does if she was mistaken for you.

'Mind if we look around?' she asked.

'Was . . . was Lucy murdered here?' Shaw queried, apprehensively.

'We don't know where Ms Brett was murdered,' Lukeson said. 'This is a location we need to confirm or rule out.'

'Then you can't have found her here. So where was she found?'

'At a place called the Old Mill. It's a pub. I believe you know of it?'

'Yes. A dive. I used to work at Mellors Service Station near the Old Mill and went there now and then for a drink. Not my scene really. Why there?'

'That's a very good question, Ms Shaw,' Andy Lukeson said.

'Sorry. I've got to go to the loo.'

A moment later, Speckle and Lukeson heard Claire Shaw's horrific scream. They rushed upstairs where they found Claire Shaw, eyes wide with terror, looking at the blood-encrusted bathroom floor and walls. In the bath, a heavy bloodstained poker with tendrils of flesh embedded in the dried blood on it, told Speckle and Lukeson that they had found the murder weapon. 'It's like a slaughterhouse!' she screamed. 'And' — she pointed to the cat lying on the landing floor, its neck at an odd angle — 'he killed Cromwell. Why would anyone do that?'

Did killing the cat mean that the animal was familiar with the killer? Or a frequent visitor to the house? In the main, cats were wary and shied away from strangers and took time to form a bond. It could be pure malice, of course; however, it could also be that the killer had not wanted to risk the cat alerting its owner to his presence. As a young girl Speckle had had a cat who would run ahead and leap up on her when a visitor came to the house. And it had been known for cats to turn viciously protective of their owners when they were threatened. A feline attack could have given Fred's victim an opportunity to retaliate or flee the house if the feline assault was determined enough. Did Fred know Claire Shaw that well? Well enough to be a regular visitor to the house; regular enough for Cromwell to have come to trust him?

Worth, Claire Shaw's lover, would fit that description, but then Worth would have known that Shaw was away, so it made no sense that he'd have come to kill her. What if Shaw had not been the intended victim? What if the assumption that Lucy Brett had been mistakenly killed for Shaw was wrong? What if all along Lucy Brett had been the victim by intent or indeed rash action? Speckle thought. There were a lot of ifs.

'I understand that you were due back from your trip to France earlier, is that right, Ms Shaw?' the DI enquired.

'Yes. But the friend I visited in Paris was taken ill with food poisoning, so I remained another day.'

198

'Did you let Lucy know of your decision?'

'Yes.'

'And Mr Worth?'

'Alistair. How do you know about Alistair?'

'Did you? Let Mr Worth know you'd be delayed returning?'

'No.'

'Why was that?'

'Well, before I left we had a . . . tiff.'

'What about?'

'That's really none of your business, Inspector,' Shaw responded curtly.

'This is a murder inquiry,' Speckle stated resolutely.

'As I said — '

'Please answer the question, Ms Shaw.'

'Alistair thought we shouldn't see each other for a while.'

'Why?'

'He's married. Getting a divorce, of course,' she added hastily. 'Alistair thought that there might be a private detective watching him.'

'It's safe to assume then that he had not informed his wife of his intention to divorce her?'

'Alistair was waiting for the right time.'

Speckle thought, half the married men in England are waiting for the right time. Mostly that time never comes.

'Look,' Shaw said, 'Alistair has nothing to

do with this. The killer must have been the man who's been in the house.'

'A man? In the house?' Lukeson checked, when it seemed Claire Shaw's statement had rattled Speckle too much to allow her to respond.

'Just little things. A dripping bathroom tap, when I was certain I had not left it dripping. Another time the toilet had been used. But again, I thought I had simply forgotten to flush it. And there was the telly guide. It had a late night, or rather an early morning film marked with a biro. It was a favourite of mine, an old black and white tear-jerker that I remembered thinking that I might wait up to watch. The odd thing is, though, that anything I might watch, I put a question mark after, not an X; an X is a must-see. At the time I just thought that I'd mixed up my codes.'

'Then one morning when I came down, there was a mug on the kitchen sink. There was a slight coffee stain in it, as if it had been rinsed and left to dry. I wouldn't have left it and thought Alistair might have, but when I asked him, he said he hadn't. At the time everything could have been just an oversight or a mistake.'

'But now . . . '

Claire Shaw hugged herself and shivered.

'Now everything is crystal clear. Lucy's

killer had been wandering about the house. I think . . . I think he was giving me little hints. Everything was so subtle and could be explained away, you see.'

DI Sally Speckle was chilled to the marrow. Lukeson cast her a sympathetic look.

'But that's silly, isn't it?' said Claire Shaw on reflection, her look tortured, her face waxen. 'Why would he want to give me hints?' Then, very quietly, 'It wasn't Lucy he wanted to murder, was it? It was me. The poor unlucky bitch was in the wrong place at the wrong time. If I hadn't selfishly begged her to housesit, she'd still be alive.'

'You can't blame yourself,' Lukeson said. 'All the wrong in this is on the side of Lucy's killer.'

'Did you report this to the police?'

'No.'

'Why not?' Lukeson queried.

'Well, what would I say? I think a tap was left dripping. I think a loo was used. Someone mucked up the telly guide. A mug had a suspicious coffee stain. That is the stuff of paranoia, isn't it?'

'If you thought you'd been broken into, there might have been fingerprints or other evidence of the intruder,' Lukeson pointed out, knowing well that it would probably have been as Shaw had said: noted and filed away.

The police could not, without definite evidence of the fact, run around to every house where someone might have imagined a break in.

'Did you mention this to Mr Worth?' Lukeson asked.

'Yes.'

'And?'

'Naturally, the last thing he'd have wanted is the attention that police all over the place would bring to the house.'

'Is the house Mr Worth's property, then?' Speckle asked, recovering. 'Not a rented property?'

'No. Alistair owns the house.'

Clearly in every situation, Worth's only concern was his own safety, Speckle thought. Two-timing bastard!

'Have you told Mr Worth of your home-coming?'

'Not yet.'

'Have you somewhere else you can stay, Ms Shaw?' Speckle asked. 'Some place you can remain out of sight until we can progress the inquiry?'

Alarm flashed in Shaw's eyes. 'Oh, God, of course. He doesn't know he's murdered the wrong woman, does he?'

'We'll need an address and phone number once you've confirmed where you'll be.'

Claire Shaw's fear became palpable. 'He'll

come after me, won't he, Inspector?'

'It's not our intention to tell him about his mistake.'

'Something like this can't be kept quiet for very long.'

That was a fact.

'I'm expecting to have him in custody quite soon,' Speckle said, with a confidence she was far from feeling.

'The killer seems to have a knowledge of your likes and dislikes, your idiosyncracies, things like using a question mark or an X on the telly guide,' Lukeson said. 'Who would know these things?'

'I can't be sure. They're not the kind of things you consciously publicize, but one could mention them in passing, but to whom and where? Well . . . ' She shrugged helplessly.

'Would Frank Mellor know?'

'That creep!' she spat. 'I wouldn't give him oxygen if his life depended on it! Was it Mellor who told you about Alistair? I bet it was. Mellor gave Alistair the evil eye every time he came to the service station. If looks could kill, Alistair would have dropped dead on the spot. Fancied his chances, Mellor,' she scoffed. 'Always touchy-feely. Made my skin crawl.'

'Did you make your feelings clear to him?' Lukeson queried.

'In no uncertain manner, Sergeant. I told him I'd prefer to kiss dog turd.'

Obviously telling people she'd prefer to kiss dog turd was Claire Shaw's standard put-down.

'Might you have told Mrs Mellor about your likes and dislikes, perhaps?' Lukeson enquired.

'Didn't have much to say to each other. We'd have a cup of coffee together now and then. She'd do most of the talking. Sarah Mellor has a compulsive disorder. She keeps checking, and checking, and checking again. She once asked me . . .'

'Yes,' Lukeson prompted, when Shaw paused, deep in thought.

' . . . if I had any odd ways. I told her how I hated dripping taps, unflushed loos, leaving unwashed crockery about — '

'Putting question marks and Xs on the telly guide?'

'Yes,' Shaw said thoughtfully. 'She might have told Mellor, mightn't she?'

'It's possible, I suppose, but don't let's jump the gun,' Andy Lukeson cautioned, when it was obvious the direction Claire Shaw's thoughts were taking. 'Did Sarah Mellor notice her husband's . . . *preoccupation* with you, Ms Shaw?'

'The day before I left, she walked in on me

204

and Mellor in the office. He'd just tried to grope me. So the atmosphere was pretty charged. And he was always hanging around me, like a dog sniffing a bitch in heat.'

'Did you leave the Mellors' employ of your own free will?'

'I was about to, but I didn't get the chance. Mellor had to go to a funeral in Leeds. He had barely driven away when Sarah Mellor told me to clear off and not to come back. And that if I ever came near her husband again' — Claire Shaw laughed, 'fat chance of that happening — she'd make certain that I'd pay a very high price.'

'Any idea of what she might have meant by that, Ms Shaw?' Speckle asked.

'No idea.'

'Was there any sign of forced entry here?'

'I never thought to check. When I moved in, Alistair had state of the art locks fitted.'

'Has the house an alarm system?'

'No. I thought it should have, but Alistair balked at the cost. Before I moved in, the house was normally rented out.'

Speckle's house, an old house, had no alarm system either. And would not have until she got the money together to have a good one fitted by a reputable company, reasoning that it would be a pure waste of money to have something fitted by a cowboy, dangerous too possibly. She wondered if the house from which Fred's latest victim came had an alarm fitted? Could it be that Fred was picking older properties without alarm systems? Locks obviously posed no problems for him, those he could ghost past.

Now with more certainty than ever, Sally Speckle knew that Fred had also been visiting her. What had happened here, had happened in her house, too.

'Does anyone else have a key to the house?' Lukeson enquired.

'Other than Alistair. No.'

'And Lucy Brett?'

'Yes, of course. How else could she have come and gone?'

'Might she have given her key to someone else? A friend, perhaps?'

Claire Shaw shook her head, 'Lucy was a very security conscious person.'

'We'll need to talk to Mr Worth,' Speckle said.

'Do you have to?'

'Yes.'

'Popping round to his front door isn't on. I told you, Alistair is married.'

'This is a murder inquiry, Ms Shaw,' Sally Speckle said tersely. 'Everything is on.'

'He hasn't done anything.'

'We haven't said that he has.'

206

'It would be unfair to involve him,' Shaw protested.

'All sorts of innocent parties get unavoidably drawn into a murder investigation,' Speckle said. 'It's a process of elimination that will hopefully lead to Ms Brett's killer. You would want her murderer caught, wouldn't you, Ms Shaw?'

Clever that, Lukeson thought. Claire Shaw could hardly say that she did not want her cousin's killer apprehended.

'Does Mr Worth have an office where we could see him?'

'Yes,' Claire Shaw said. Then, enthusiastically, 'But I have a better idea. You could see him at his club. Away from prying eyes and office gossip.'

'Very well,' Speckle agreed.

'I'll phone and set things up, shall I?'

If Sally Speckle was of a mind to object, it was already too late, because Shaw had her lover's number ringing. 'Darling . . . ' She stepped into the bedroom adjacent to the bathroom to continue the conversation, but was not bold enough to shut the door. However, her conversation was from the far end of the bedroom and whispered. Her chat was brief, and when she returned she said uneasily, 'Alistair's agreed to meet you.'

An agreement, judging by the duration and

animated nature of the call, that clearly had not been a willing one.

'How soon can you leave, Ms Shaw? We'll need to get Scene of Crime Officers in here right away. The crime scene is already old.'

'Right away, I suppose.'

'Do you know who fitted the new locks when you moved in?' Lukeson enquired.

'Ah . . . I have a receipt somewhere.'

'Mind having a look?'

Claire Shaw left the room.

'You're scared, aren't you, boss?' Sally Speckle's troubled look confirmed Andy Lukeson's suspicions. 'Fred likes to make himself at home, doesn't he? Uses the loo. Makes coffee. Watches telly.'

'You know what, Andy,' Speckle said thoughtfully. 'I think that's part of his game. He's telling his victims that he's been in their homes, only in a subtle way.'

'The point being?'

Speckle shrugged. 'Maybe if you tumble to his game, the prize might be to let you be? Perhaps if you tumble to what is going on, he'll consider you his equal in intellect? Most killers, the cold-blooded variety at any rate, have a superiority complex, an ego, the kind of ego that might reward a victim he considered intelligent — as intelligent as himself.'

208

Lukeson's acceptance of the theory was lukewarm.

'What about Worth?' he said. 'Maybe Shaw's delay in returning threw his plans out of sync. He came round, whacked Lucy by mistake. Brett being a look-a-like, it's easy to see how a mistake could be made at the best of times. But, tense and edgy, wanting to get it over with quickly . . . '

'After that first devastating blow, I reckon most of Lucy Brett's face was gone anyway. By the second blow, she was unrecognizable.'

'Lucy Brett was struck down in Shaw's bathrobe coming out of the bathroom; that means that she was ready for bed and she'd have put off the downstairs lights. Worth must not have put on any lights, because had he, she'd have been immediately cautious on opening the bathroom door.'

'A clinging lover, is a common enough motive for murder.'

'But why would Worth be creeping about the house, Andy?'

'To set the scene for when he topped Shaw.'

'But wouldn't he let Shaw report it to the police, if he wanted to set the scene?'

'He didn't want to attract attention to the house with a suspicious wife in the wings. When Shaw was murdered, he could come forward with the story about the creeper. With any luck, she'd have mentioned it to someone else, too. And Worth would have known Shaw's idiosyncracies.'

'But if his intention was to rid himself of the problem of a lover, having a woman murdered in a house he owns wouldn't help. Worth would have all the attention he could ever want, Andy. And what if Shaw had also, along with mentioning someone creeping about the house, told someone that she was Worth's lover?'

'Fanciful thinking on her part,' Lukeson suggested. 'But the point would be that with Shaw dead, Worth could tell whatever story he liked.'

'I can't really see it working, Andy,' Speckle said honestly.

Arriving back in the room, Claire Shaw said, in response to Lukeson's query about who had fitted the locks, 'I couldn't find the receipt, but I'm petty sure that it was Melchett's.'

'In Loston?' Speckle enquired. 'I can't place them?'

'They've been around about five years,' Lukeson said. 'Used to be Stratton's.'

'Bert Stratton?'

'That Stratton. He of the fondness for other people's goods. The best cat-burglar in the business. Got caught once, in what was thought to be at least a twenty-year career. His nickname was 'The Ghost', because he could come and go as quietly as one. But before you get all excited, boss, Stratton had a heart attack while inside and croaked.'

'Pity.'

'Yes, indeed. Because Bert Stratton was a vicious sod, and if he was still around, in him we'd have had a very interesting suspect.'

'I checked with Nicole, my friend,' Shaw said 'It's OK to stay. I've phoned for a cab. The address and phone number.' She handed Speckle a piece of paper.

'Thanks. And it would be best if you remained indoors for the time being,' Speckle said. 'We'll keep you updated on progress.'

DS Andy Lukeson had been in deep thought.

'Ms Shaw what kind of arrangement with Mr Worth do you have regarding your occupancy of the house?'

'I'm not sure I understand, Sergeant?'

Neither did Sally Speckle.

'Do you live here at Alistair Worth's generosity?'

'I pay rent.' Claire Shaw laughed. 'In a way.'

'Now it's my turn to be confused,' Lukeson said, with a smile.

'Alistair thought that it would be safer for

me to appear to be a tenant. Otherwise, his wife would, of course, wonder about my being here. So Alistair came up with a rather clever arrangement. I would pay the rent, as a tenant, and he would refund me the money.'

'That is clever,' Lukeson said.

You crafty bastard Andy Lukeson, Sally Speckle thought.

As the cab pulled away, Lukeson said, 'Isn't our Mr Worth a clever lad, boss? When Shaw's body would have been found, he'd have lost a tenant and not dealt with a problem. It might be an idea to check on Worth's movements when that phone call was made to you.'

'I've a question, Andy.'

'I thought you might have. Go on, then.'

'Why would Worth go to all the trouble of inventing Fred, if all that had happened was that his tenant had been topped?'

DS Andy Lukeson grimaced.

'Question number two.'

'You're loving this, aren't you?' Andy said.

'How would Worth get his hands on a patient's dressing-gown?'

'He could buy a green dressing-gown?'

'With LMH in bold letters on the back of it?'

'Don't crow,' Lukeson grumbled.

'You know, Andy,' Speckle said reflectively,

'if we had even a smidgen of answers instead of a mountain of questions, we'd have this case solved. Andy — '

'Don't think so hard,' he said, when Speckle frowned. 'You'll get wrinkles.'

'What if Sarah Mellor is a killer by proxy?'

'Go on.'

'What if she hired a hitman?'

'A hitman? Loston isn't Chicago. Where would she find one?'

'Oh, not a pro. Some tearaway who'd cut his mother's throat for a fix. She'd have been able to arrange the hospital end of things.'

'And this tearaway would be prepared to go on killing women to give credence to Fred?' queried Andy sceptically.

'Why not?'

'Question.'

'You're a tosser, Andy. I thought there might be.'

'Why invent Fred in the first place? Why not simply have this tearaway murder Shaw and leave it at that?'

'Hide the murder within murders? Frank Mellor was trying it on with Shaw. She's topped. A furious and jealous wife would be looked at very seriously. But if Shaw was one of . . . '

On hearing about the gruesome discovery at Speckle's house, DC Charlie Johnson was left with only one strand of inquiry regarding Benny Frederics, and that was the assault on the old-age pensioner on Sykes Street. As he'd been in custody at the time, he could not have murdered the woman found in DI Sally Speckle's armchair.

16

Feeling incredibly exhilarated by the woman's murder and the dumping of her body in Speckle's house, Fred was outside Alice Mulgrave's house when she came out the next morning. He had been unable to rest, so intense had his desire to kill again become. At first he was stunned. But then he saw how killing the woman he had followed from the park was absolutely the perfect thing to do. It could not be more fitting if he had planned it.

The gods were with him!

He watched from the stolen Micra (his plan to steal what he wanted, cars, mobiles etc, had been a wise one, he thought), as the uniformed woman drove away. He was no expert in reading the insignia of rank, but he knew that she was close to the top of the copper pyramid.

What a prize. What a present for DI Sally Speckle.

Fred's exhilaration knew no bounds now. He would break into the house and wait until the top copper arrived back home. When she left, he could hardly contain his excitement, wanting to dash across the road and break into the house immediately, but he needed to get rid of the car. Parked, a passing squaddie could spot it, and it would not take long for someone to mention that a top copper was living on the street which would, in these terrorist threatened times, have police swarming all over the place. And the Micra would be crawling with trace evidence, so, like the Fiesta, burning was best. A rag in the petrol tank was an old trick he'd learned in his joyriding days. Having never been caught the trick had proved successful.

Sometimes he felt that he had made the wrong decision in becoming what he now was, even for Mary, his girlfriend. Having studied under his stepfather Bert Stratton, a life of crime would have been the logical career. There wasn't a lock that Stratton could not open in seconds flat. As a locksmith, he had fitted locks to most places he had burgled. He had spare keys, but had never used them, preferring instead to open the lock without using a key, a skill he had passed on to his stepson, which was about the only useful thing he had passed on. May the bastard rot in hell. But he supposed that eventually one found one's true calling. He had. Killing women. God, he was so looking forward to the pleasure ahead that it made him quite breathless.

It would be the most perfect day of his life.

* * *

Getting into the lift on her way to CS Doyle's office, Sally Speckle's mobile rang. 'Yes,' she said impatiently, conscious of time, having been late for her first meeting with Alice Mulgrave. 'Morning, Helen,' she said. 'I am really pushed for time right now . . . Good work. Get round to check it out. Take Brian with you.'

'Something new?' Lukeson asked.

'Helen Rochester has dug up something I'd completely forgotten about. When I was a rookie and no one really knew what to do with me, I went on a call out to a house in Worthington Avenue, a posh name for a very grotty little street, to deal with a serious assault. A woman had attacked another woman with a knitting needle, because she was wearing an identical dress, and her assailant had got it into her head that this neighbour was upstaging her on purpose. The frocks were on sale at a local store and were a penny a dozen. Mary Alcott was the woman's name, not much more than a girl really, with a history of paranoid schizophrenia. She had stuck the knitting needle into her neighbour's right eye. Luckily it had not penetrated too far. But she did lose the sight in that eye. Mary Alcott was arrested and later sectioned to a facility near Birmingham.'

217

'Could be the motive behind all of this,' Lukeson said. 'Had Alcott family?'

'Yes. Mother, father, three brothers. But they understood that she needed to be sectioned for her own good. In fact, in follow up, they were relieved. At least they appeared to be. Helen is on her way to Worthington Avenue to talk to the Alcotts.'

'You were a rookie?'

'Greener than spring leaves.'

'With the powerful medicine nowadays, Mary Alcott must have got out ages ago. But, of course, medication only works if it's taken.'

'But Mary Alcott couldn't be Fred, Andy.'

'But she could have met Fred along the way, and poured out her heart to him about this bitch of a copper who was responsible for all her woes. He gets out and decides to make life miserable for you.'

'But I had nothing to do with having her sectioned.'

'It's hard to be objective when you're mentally ill,' Lukeson said. 'You arrested her, so he believes you must have had her sectioned.'

★ ★ ★

DC Helen Rochester and PC Brian Scuttle stood looking at what had formerly been

218

Worthington Avenue, which was now a weed-filled site awaiting redevelopment.

'The council should know where the Alcotts were relocated to,' Scuttle said.

'Look,' Rochester pointed.

At the far end of the street there was still one house standing defiantly in the rubble all round it. A moment later, responding to Rochester's summons, an elderly man opened the shabby door of the house and immediately said, 'Wonder when you lot would turn up. So I'll tell you what I told them what come from the council. This has been my home for seventy-one years and I ain't budgin'! Not one flamin' inch! So do what you want about it.'

The door slammed shut.

Rochester knocked again. The man appeared at a window and shouted something they could not hear, but there was no disguising its uncomplimentary nature.

Scuttle went to the window and barked, 'Open the door, you silly old git!'

The man opened the top half of the sash window and shouted back, 'Bastards, one an' all!'

'The council didn't send us,' Rochester said placatingly, cutting across PC Scuttle's intended angry riposte, and in an aside told Scuttle, 'Give it a rest, Brian!'

'Hah!' the old man scoffed.

'It's true, Mr . . . ?'

'Name's Abbot. Sid Abbot. Sick, that is. You don't even bother findin' out the name of the person you Nazi bastards have come to kick out. Named you lot well when they called you pigs, eh.'

'Look, Mr Abbot, we've come to ask you about a neighbour of yours, that's all,' Helen Rochester said, by now straining at the leash along with Scuttle.

'Neighbours!' he scoffed. 'You blind, girl? Ain't no neighbours, is there?'

'Former neighbours, Mr Abbot. The Alcotts.'

'Long gone, the Alcotts. And good riddance, I say. With that loony daughter of theirs goin' about doin' mischief all the time. Stickin' knitting needles in people's eyes. A right one, was Mary Alcott. Batty since the day she popped outa her mother's belly, she was.'

'Do you know where the council might have relocated them to, Mr Abbot?' Rochester enquired.

'Why don't you ask the council, and not be botherin' me?'

'We can do that, of course, Mr Abbot,' Rochester said, not sure of how long more she could keep her patience. 'But now that we're here, we thought you might know and want to help the police.'

He cackled. 'Want to help the police? Would a Jew want to go to dinner with Adolf Hitler? Don't be daft, woman.'

Abbot closed the window and vanished from it.

They were leaving when the front door opened.

'Devon,' Sid Abbot said. 'That's where the Alcotts went. Shirl Alcott come from Devon. Some relation of hers popped her clogs, left her the house. So once they found out that the Social was the same in Devon as it is here, they upped and left, the lot of 'em. Lazy sods, one an' all, the Alcotts.'

'Do you know where in Devon they have gone to, Mr Abbot?' Helen Rochester enquired.

'Coppers ain't meant to be that shape,' he said to Scuttle. 'Disturbin', that.' And to Rochester, 'Wha' d'ya think I am, eh? They left and that was that.'

'OK,' Scuttle said, exasperated, 'Can you tell us, did Mary Alcott move with the rest of the family?'

'Naw. She weren't 'round, was she. Locked up in the loony bin, was Mary.'

'So do you know where she is now?'

Sid Abbot's eyes took in every inch of Helen Rochester.

'Do nights together, d'ya?' he enquired of Scuttle. He laughed. 'Maybe I should've been

221

a copper instead of a thief, eh?'

DC Helen Rochester hated the old man's lecherous eyes on her, but she took consolation in the fact that her latest diet had worked. And all she had to do now was avoid the canteen's sticky buns.

'Do you know where Mary Alcott is now?' Scuttle asked again. 'And, if you could do anything about it, you'd be a dirty old man, Sid Abbot.'

Rochester winced. Would Brian Scuttle ever learn when a shut mouth was best? However, Sid Abbot laughed, and became the very essence of joviality.

'Got a picture of Marilyn Monroe on the wall 'bove me bed. One glance and I sleep happily.'

'Good for you, Sid,' Scuttle said. 'Bit before my time, though.'

'Now there was a woman. All curves. Not a titless stick like nowadays. Loston Mental, o' course.'

'Mary Alcott is in Loston Mental Hospital?' Rochester checked, astonished.

'Used to call them places asylums in my day,' Abbot said. 'Nowadays they give everythin' fancy names to hide what they truly are. Now, you tell them jackboot queers at the council that I'm stayin' put!'

The front door slammed shut.

17

'Come in.'

DI Sally Speckle took a deep breath before entering CS Doyle's office. Alice Mulgrave was standing, looking out the window with her back to Speckle. The Chief Super had the stony expression he always wore when unpleasant news needed to be conveyed.

'Ma'am,' Speckle greeted the Assistant Chief Constable. 'Sir.'

Frank Doyle scowled, his gaze going to the wall clock.

'Inspector. How are you today?' Mulgrave enquired, adding her glance to Doyle's towards the wall clock. 'I heard there was quite a shock awaiting you when you got home last night.'

'I've had more pleasant homecomings, ma'am.' Mulgrave's gaze went to Doyle and then back to Speckle, as she went and sat alongside Doyle — a coming together of authority, Speckle thought. In her experience, always ominous.

Sally Speckle turned her full attention to the CS, because that was where she was now certain that bad news would come from.

'Sit down, Inspector,' Doyle said. Once Speckle was seated, the Chief Super continued, 'This wrong identity business is disturbing, isn't it.'

'Disturbing, but understandable, sir,' Speckle said.

The lines on his face bunched together in a grimace. 'An identity based on a tattoo. Not very scientific, is it, Speckle?'

Doyle, whom she knew as a relatively calm man, seemed unusually exasperated.

'The tattoo was quite distinctive,' Speckle said by way of defence. 'The victim had no face left to identify her by, and science takes time to reach a conclusion, longer still,' she said pointedly, 'when the science is, like every other branch of policing, under-resourced, sir. So, rather than everyone sitting round waiting, I thought it better to make a start.'

'Unfortunately, Inspector, there is not a bottomless pit of money available,' Mulgrave chipped in. 'And what there is has to be spent with prudent wisdom.'

'Of course, ma'am,' Speckle agreed. 'However, if resources are scarce, then one can only do one's best with what's available. Wouldn't you agree, ma'am?'

Though Doyle would gladly have wrung her neck, he admired Speckle's unwillingness to be cowed.

If the stony silence from the ACC held for

much longer, Speckle was fearful that Doyle would forget how to draw breath.

DI Sally Speckle had a sense that the skirmish was a precursor to something more devastating to come. She was right. Mulgrave's glance the Chief Super's way, was the prompt to break the bad news that was to come. And, true to form, Frank Doyle took no prisoners.

'With two murders in quick succession, and the probability of more to come, it's time to call in the RCS.'

Sally Speckle was stunned.

'I respectfully suggest that there's no need to call in the Regional Crime Squad, sir,' she protested. 'I have every confidence that we can catch this killer.'

'After what body count, Inspector?' Mulgrave intoned.

'I must place on record my objection, ma'am,' Speckle said tersely. 'I believe the decision to call in the RCS is premature and unfair to officers who have a proven track record.'

Doyle's rebuke was swift. 'That'll be quite enough, Speckle.'

Alice Mulgrave studied Sally Speckle.

'A moment ago, Inspector, you cited lack of resources as an impediment. Well, the RCS will have those resources available to them.

Therefore should you not be supportive of their taking over this investigation? After all, it's the arrest of this killer that's important, not local noses that might be put out of joint.'

Incensed, and not giving a damn, Speckle said, 'I can only say, ma'am, that if the RCS is called in I shall take it as a comment on me, personally. I should therefore have to consider resigning.'

'Is this an attempt to put a gun to my head, Inspector?' Mulgrave asked, quietly.

'No, ma'am. It is not.'

'I should hope not, Speckle,' Doyle barked.

'I don't intend to change my mind,' Mulgrave said, resolutely. 'Now, is it still your wish to resign, Inspector?'

Mulgrave had taken a line Speckle had hoped she would not, but she had opened the door, so now she must accept the outcome.

'With due respect, ma'am, and more to the point, is it your wish?' Speckle said.

Frank 'Sermon' Doyle was gobsmacked. He shot Speckle a *don't push your luck too far* look, without much hope, based on past experience of Speckle heeding his advice. He admired her grit, but not her stupidity. She had backed Mulgrave into a corner, and corners were not places that senior officers liked to be pushed into.

'Inspector Speckle. I am cognisant of your

views, opinions and objections,' Mulgrave said. 'I hope you are equally cognisant of my duty to do what I deem necessary to achieve the best result all round. A right you insisted on when choosing a suitable officer to stand in for DS Lukeson when he was away on a course.'

ACC Alice Mulgrave was not shy about putting in the boot, Doyle thought. Come on, woman, be sensible, Doyle prayed. You've fought the good fight. Now let it be.

As the seconds dragged on, Doyle began to fear that his prayers were not going to be answered. Then, surprisingly, it was Alice Mulgrave who conceded ground.

'I would like to think, Inspector Speckle, that you will have a long and I'm sure a very distinguished career ahead of you. But, of course, the choice is yours.'

Doyle thought, take the bloody olive branch, Sally. It's not often a senior officer will hold one out.

'I hope I can justify your confidence in me, ma'am,' Speckle said, to Frank Doyle's immense relief.

'I have no doubt that you will, Inspector,' Alice Mulgrave said, and lost not a second in re-establishing their respective ranks. 'When DCI Amber arrives with the RCS team in a couple of days, I will expect the maximum co-operation with the least resistance, Inspector. Is that understood?'

'Ma'am.'

'You're a fine police officer, and a very able DI,' Mulgrave said. 'And I have no doubt at all that, given time, you would catch Fred, but time is not a commodity we have much of, if this killer fulfils anything like the potential he has shown.'

Now Sally Speckle knew how Charlie Johnson must have felt when she had side-lined him, and the medicine was bitter to swallow. She had to accept Mulgrave's right to pick the personnel she thought most suited to the task in hand. However, such reasonable logic and understanding did nothing to assuage her anger.

The same anger Charlie Johnson must have felt with her.

'That's all, Speckle,' Doyle said, quick to end the meeting and avoid any renewal of hostilities. In his long experience it was when a resolution to a dispute had been found, that it was at its most likely to slip away as pride reasserted itself.

'Yes, sir,' Speckle said. 'Ma'am.'

'Good day, Inspector.'

★ ★ ★

'What!' Andy Lukeson barked five minutes later, when Speckle told him of Mulgrave's decision. 'We get all the donkey work, and the RCS gets all the glory!'

'It'll take a couple of days for the RCS to put in an appearance. Until then, Andy, it's still our case. So let's make the Regional Crime Squad redundant before they start, and nail this bastard Fred! Let's make sure that by the time the RCS arrive, all they'll have to do is put the pink ribbon on the parcel.'

They had arrived outside the briefing room.

'So let's get on with it, shall we?'

★　★　★

Rochester brought the team up to speed on her and Scuttle's encounter with Sid Abbot. 'A bit of a bombshell,' Rochester said. 'Mary Alcott, the possible motive for all of this, being right here in Loston Mental Hospital.'

'Good work, Helen,' Speckle complimented her. 'You too, Brian.'

'I was only along to make up the numbers,' he said sullenly, obviously seeing his compliment as a necessary tag on.

'And not very good company at that,' Lukeson said.

'I do my bit, Sarge,' Scuttle responded. 'I didn't think I'd have to go Ho-Ho-Ho as well.'

WPC Anne Fenning said, 'Jack Ansome never was a priest, but he was a seminarian. However, he was kicked out when a cleaner found nasty photographs in his room and reported him to his superiors.'

She gave them details of what Ansome had done to the photographs.

'Seems Ansome was on a mission to punish women whom he thought were harlots, doesn't it?' Charlie Johnson said.

'They quickly alerted other orders, seminaries and parishes to Ansome, and that was the end of that.'

'He could have gone abroad,' Rochester said.

'Unlikely. After troubled times in the past, the Roman Catholic church is getting its act very much together. And, according to Father Lake, the alert about Ansome would be very far reaching.'

'Still, Ansome could be our man. A thwarted cleric with an exaggerated sense of morality. God only knows what kind of a fantasy world he lives in,' Johnson said.

'Ansome was always my favourite to be Fred,' Rochester said.

'Female intuition,' Brian Scuttle snorted.

'Ansome by all accounts was a crotchety git, but then so are a lot of people.' He sighed. 'Including me. Sorry, everyone.'

There was a moment in which no one seemed to know what to say, before Sally Speckle spoke. 'Charlie, anything yet on Judy Mayhew?'

'She hasn't returned to her beat,' the DC reported. 'And there's no reply from her flat.'

'How long has she been missing?' The question was Lukeson's.

'Varies. Some of the women say it's been a fortnight or more. And others say that it's no more than a week.'

'Has anyone, in the house where she lives, seen her?'

'No.'

'No one's bothered to check on her?'

'Mayhew apparently keeps herself to herself. Cut yourself off, and people soon forget you exist. And if they do remember, they won't want to be told to mind their own business if they enquire.'

'What happened to neighbourliness?' Lukeson said.

'This is the age of individualism, Andy,' Anne Fenning said. 'People just don't want to get involved as people did in more innocent times.'

'Maybe it's time to have a look inside Judy

Mayhew's flat,' Speckle said. Her voice conveyed a troubled spirit, the explanation for which came in her next utterance. 'What if Mayhew has been one of Fred's victims?'

'But if Fred killed Mayhew wouldn't he, true to form, have put her some place for you to find, guv?' Fenning pointed out.

'That would seem logical,' Speckle conceded. 'But madness and logic aren't compatible. And maybe he's keeping Judy Mayhew on ice.'

'Mary Alcott was sectioned,' Lukeson said. 'The boss was involved in the incident which led to her being sectioned. So my money is on that incident to provide a motive. I think Fred is in some way connected to Mary Alcott, a family member, maybe.'

'Has Abbot any idea where in Devon the Alcotts are?' Fenning asked.

'He's no idea,' Rochester answered.

'What about Mellor?' Fenning asked. 'Unrequited love and all that?'

Speckle brought the team up to speed on her and Lukeson's interview with Claire Shaw.

'This fellow Worth seems a possible, doesn't he?' Rochester said.

'Certainly worth looking into,' Speckle said. 'If you'll pardon the pun. Fred seems to ghost his way past locks. So check the backgrounds of every suspect to find out if they ever worked or trained as a locksmith.'

'And there's a suspicion, my suspicion to be precise,' Speckle said, 'that he enters houses without alarms fitted. That would be mostly older houses that would cost an arm and a leg to wire up.'

'Talking of locks,' Fenning said. 'I phoned Melchett's. The fitter who did Shaw's locks was killed in a car accident a couple of weeks ago. Didn't have a mate. Self-employed. Worked on contract.'

'At least it's one less we won't have to give time to,' Lukeson said.

Speckle instructed, 'Anne, check back with the church authorities. Dig some more about Ansome. Talk to the cleaner who found the pictures. If she's not still with the order, get her address and go round.'

'Charlie get on to uniform to raid Judy Mayhew's flat.'

'Search warrant?'

'It's in her and the public's interest that we break into Mayhew's flat. The public would quickly accuse us of negligence if she were ill and we did nothing about it. Brian, anything on Loston's gyms?'

'Nothing.'

'Well, it was a longshot. Help out where you're needed. OK?'

Obviously Scuttle did not appreciate a dogsbody's role, but it was part and parcel of teamwork. Next time round, it would fall to someone else.

'Helen, get along to the renal clinic at Loston General Hospital. I don't know what you'll be hoping to uncover or discover, but the clinic has come up for mention a couple of times. Frank Mellor told Andy that he learned about Claire Shaw and Worth's movements from a nurse at the clinic she was friendly with. Talk to the nurse.'

'Anything from forensics on the Mellor station wagon?' Johnson asked.

'Nothing so far,' Speckle said. 'Charlie, I need someone to bring all the threads together to form some kind of a pattern. That's you.'

'Andy, you and I will try and talk to Mary Alcott. We can take in Worth on the way. Just one more thing: the ACC has decided to call in the Regional Crime Squad.'

A collective howl went up. Some angry views were voiced about Alice Mulgrave's decision.

'It's a right kick in the arse!' Scuttle said.

'To me,' Speckle said, catching DC Charlie Johnson's eye, 'not to you.'

A glum mood settled over the team, and Speckle wondered if she might have been wiser to have witheld word of the RCS moving in until they were virtually knocking on the door. She hoped it would not affect the team's resolve to bring Fred to justice.

'Right,' she said in a rallying tone of voice. 'We can sit here all day and speculate as to what happened and who made it happen, but we won't be much further along the road. So let's do what coppers do best. Ask questions and get answers.'

DI Sally Speckle sighed wearily. At the present rate of progress the file she would be handing over to the Regional Crime Squad would be a very slim one indeed. When the team dispersed, Speckle asked Lukeson, 'Do you ever feel like just walking out, Andy? Packing it all in?'

'A couple of times a day,' he replied. 'But to do what? There's not much you can do when being a copper is all you know.'

'It'll be a right kick in the teeth if we have to hand over to the RCS.'

'It can always be worse than it is, my mum used to say,' Lukeson said.

Speckle's phone rang. 'Speckle . . . Right. Thanks.' She broke the connection. 'Could it, Andy?' she said by way of reply to what his mum used to say. 'No prints on the murder weapon. And not a sliver of evidence in the Mellor station wagon either.'

18

The back door lock was too easy. Fred liked his locks to be a challenge. When they weren't, all that knowledge that his no-good stepfather Bert Stratton (ace locksmith and even better burglar) had passed on about locks of all shapes and sizes and how they could be opened without a key was wasted. Letting himself into the kitchen of 8 Crescent Road, the top copper's house, Fred stood listening. The house was perfectly still. Looking about the kitchen, he saw immediately that he might be in Sally Speckle's house, everything neat and dusted and in its proper place. He made his way along the hall to the sitting-room, certain that he would find the sofa cushions fluffed. He was right. What was it about coppers and neatness? Probably all that checking and rechecking every little detail became a practice that overflowed into their private lives. Preoccupied, he did not notice the dog basket behind an armchair by the fireplace, and only became aware of the poodle when it barked, a second before it sank its teeth into his leg. Grimacing with the pain of the dog bite, Fred swung around and kicked the poodle, sending it flying. He grabbed the stunned dog, marched to the kitchen, placed the whimpering poodle in the microwave, slammed the door shut, and switched it on. 'Told you what I'd do to you,' Fred said and, laughing, left the kitchen.

Slowly and carefully he went through the house, pausing along the way to get a sense of his next victim, but he could not pick up any vibes. There was nothing that he could see of its owner. A cold house, lacking any personal touch. A house between owners? he wondered. A house caught between the fading presence of its previous occupant, and the, as yet, unestablished ambience of its new dweller.

He checked the bathroom; bathrooms were great revealers of secrets and personality, like the condoms in Claire Shaw's bathroom. The male deodorant that first alerted him to Alistair Worth. A pair of tooth brushes was another pointer, one dried out, which told him of the male's irregular residency, conclusion — a lover.

He sniffed at what he would decribe as a *sensible* perfume, its scent discreet, designed, Fred reckoned, for polite social occasions as opposed to a brash fragrance, intended to attract males. As he progressed, he saw repeated, many of the signs he had observed in Speckle's house. What he would describe as the seeds of spinster-hood.

A careful man, Fred took nothing for granted. He checked every nook and cranny of the house until he was absolutely satisfied that the woman lived alone. No need here for little teasing hints of his presence, as he had left in Shaw and Speckle's houses. He'd be waiting for his next victim when she came home.

He laughed slyly.

'A murdered top copper should put the cat among the pigeons, Sally.'

⋆ ⋆ ⋆

'You looked displeased, Chief Superintendent,' Alice Mulgrave observed, when Speckle had left the meeting.

CS Frank Doyle did not mince his words. 'I am, ma'am. I don't believe it's necessary to call in the Regional Crime Squad. Sally Speckle is a fine officer, and heads up an equally fine team. I have no doubt at all that, given time, they would have — '

'Given time,' Mulgrave interjected. 'How many dead women would constitute *given time?*'

'The RCS won't have a magic wand to wave either,' Doyle said tersely, not prepared to give ground.

'They'll have access to resources such as profilers, Chief Superintendent.'

'If we needed that kind of expertise, we could have had it drafted in, ma'am.'

Assistant Chief Constable Alice Mulgrave locked eyes with Doyle, neither prepared to flinch.

'I think the air between us needs to be cleared, Chief Superintendent.' Mulgrave's tone, while not aggressive or condescending, held a note of rank. 'It's my opinion that you think I've called in the RCS to be seen to be doing something. A new broom and all that. Conscious of the media. And, of course, trying to justify my recent and, frankly, quite unexpected promotion.'

Frank Doyle said nothing.

'I'll admit that if I were you, I would be tempted to think the same. However, it is not true. And hopefully, in time, you will come to see me in a better light than you do now.'

'Ma'am,' Doyle replied, neutrally. He steered the conversation on to a less contentious topic. 'Settling into the house, are you, ma'am?'

'Yes. With your brother-in-law away in America for a year, it will give me time to decide on where I shall finally settle. I must thank you again for arranging it for me. I've taken several walks in the nearby park.' She frowned. 'Any trouble there, Chief Superintendent?' she enquired, conscious of the man whom she had thought followed her.

'Not really. At least nothing serious. Though there was an incident where a duck was set alight.'

'Anyone caught for this?'

'No. A burned duck would be a long way down the line of priorities, ma'am.'

'You know, sometimes I think that were the acts of vandalism which are considered to be of the lower order given more attention, it might prevent, later, the more serious crimes of people who go around setting ducks alight.'

She stood up.

'Now, I really must be getting along.' She paused in the open door. 'Oh, just before I take my leave, it's come to my attention that Loston's somewhat over budget, Chief Superintendent.'

'Policing nowadays doesn't come cheaply,' Doyle said in his defence.

'Indeed,' Mulgrave agreed. 'However, as far as Loston goes, it doesn't have to cost as much as sending a shuttle into space either.'

'Any suggestions, ma'am?' Doyle invited stiffly.

'I'm sure you don't need me to point out where cuts in expenditure might be achieved.

Until the next time, Chief Superintendent.'

Frank 'Sermon' Doyle, wished he was nearer his pension. A nice little villa in Lanzarotte, nothing too fancy, was a dream he now wished in reality.

19

'Inspector Speckle?' Sally Speckle turned to look at the man who was standing off to the side of the main entrance to Alistair Worth's club, and guessed who he was before he introduced himself. 'I thought we might talk in my car, Inspector.' He pointed to a sleek, black Mercedes in the forecourt of the very posh club. 'It would be infinitely more private.' He looked to Lukeson for support, but not getting any felt compelled to explain, 'It's my father-in-law, you see. Julius Herbert Bracken. He's inside. Rather a sticky wicket. He dotes on his daughter, Sarah, my wife.'

Julius Herbert Bracken had more pies than he had fingers, counted ten times over, to put in. Which meant that when money was needed (the kind of money needed to build business empires) quite a number of paths led to the door of Bracken's private bank. Not at all the kind of father-in-law a chap would want to upset if he wished to have three square meals a day, Andy Lukeson thought, not withstanding the fact that by reputation, Julius Herbert Bracken was a very kindly man whose considerable fortune had been

242

acquired by honest hard work.

'A very powerful and influential man,' Speckle observed.

'Yes. He is.'

Lukeson thought, if Bracken finds out you've been playing away from home, me old son, you're dog meat. Not that he'd lose any sleep over Worth, the selfish, toffee-nosed prat.

Considering his request consented to — he'd be used to having his every wish granted, no doubt — Alistair Worth walked ahead to the Mercedes.

'Are you going to be led by the nose by that stuffed shirt?' Lukeson protested, when Speckle went to follow.

'Is that a red flag you're waving, Andy,' she responded narkily. 'If Worth can in the least way help us to catch Fred, I'd get into a wheelie bin with him. Now come on!'

'Maybe he is Fred,' Lukeson said soberly. The cautionary note struck, brought Speckle up short for a moment. 'Don't assume that because he doesn't come from a place like the Clewbridge, that underneath the posh and dosh he's not rotten.'

'Any other wisdoms you might think fitting to an officer you obviously think needs her social conscience pricked, Sergeant?'

'Just offering advice, ma'am,' Lukeson

responded stiffly. 'But I promise to try harder to button my lip.'

Sally Speckle smiled. 'You can be a thorny devil, Andy.'

'Likewise, ma'am.'

'I'm not your mother. So less of the ma'am. Now, come on.'

Settled in the sumptious Merc, Worth said, 'A terrible business.'

'Murder always is,' Lukeson said sharply.

'How is Claire?' Worth asked.

'Haven't you been round?' Lukeson enquired.

'Well, no. I have to be very careful, you understand. Claire said she explained.'

Andy Lukeson thought, what a ponce you are Mr Worth.

'The thing is, that I've decided to end the relationship.' He shrugged. 'These things run their course.'

'How do you think she'll take it?' Lukeson asked. 'Kick up a bit of a fuss, maybe? Mad as hell that she's being given the elbow probably.'

'Naturally, these situations can be somewhat acrimonious, Sergeant. But Claire is a sensible girl.'

'You're hoping,' Lukeson said.

'I'm sure she'll realize that all our relationship amounted to was a fling,' he said coldly.

'I doubt it. Not after you told her that you

244

were getting a divorce,' Andy Lukeson stated bluntly.

'Pillow talk. That's all that was.'

Worth was unfazed by Andy Lukeson's very obvious dislike of him.

DI Sally Speckle thought how true the adage about taking the book by the cover, or the man by his appearance was. Rats, she had met in her time, but none bigger nor more ugly than Alistair Worth would she ever find again, she reckoned.

'Aren't you afraid she'll tell your wife?' Lukeson asked. Worth paled. 'Worse still, your father-in-law?' There was more colour in white paint than there was on Worth's face. 'A difficult situation, that. A man might be prepared to do a lot to avoid it.'

'What do you mean?' Worth asked sharply, already knowing full well what Lukeson was saying.

'Ms Shaw told us that she did not inform you that she would be delayed in returning from France. Correct?'

'Yes.'

'So, expecting that she'd be at home, perhaps you went round to have a . . . chat?'

'No. I thought it best to let things quieten down.'

'Did you know that Ms Shaw had a housesitter?' Lukeson continued.

'No. I wouldn't have approved.'

'Why not?'

'One doesn't like strangers walking all over one's property, does one?'

'I wouldn't know, Mr Worth. I don't have any property for strangers to walk all over.'

Finally goaded, Worth held Lukeson's gaze.

'Look, let's shorten this for all our sakes. You're' — he included Speckle in his perusal — 'thinking that here is a man with a lover who could, if she were bloody-minded, ruin everything for him. So in a bit of a panic, he pops round and removes the problem. Right?'

'Concisely put, Mr Worth,' Speckle said. 'Did you remove the problem?'

'I'm a financier, Inspector. I suck someone's blood every day, but seldom to the point of their extinction, no profit in that. But I am not a murderer. If Claire decides to become a whistle blower, then I'll have to suffer the consequences of my folly.'

Worth checked his gold Rolex.

'Is that it? I'm pressed for time.'

'We may wish to speak to you again,' Speckle said.

'Can't see why. However, next time, if there is a next time, I suggest that any talking be done at my solicitor's office.'

Walking back to Speckle's clapped-out Punto, Andy Lukeson said, 'An affair gone

246

sour and a clinging woman is a classic motive for murder. And he was quick to involve his solicitor, don't you think?'

'Not unusual, if you have a solicitor on a retainer, as Worth would have. And the woman in my sitting-room? Where does she fit in?'

DS Andy Lukeson's response was a hunch of his shoulders.

'And that all important dressing-gown. How would Worth get hold of one?'

'Desperate needs makes for desperate deeds,' was Lukeson's somewhat lame reply. 'The fact is, that Worth will be out on his ear and ruined if he gets on the wrong side of Julius Herbert Bracken. And cheating on his favourite daughter is surely the way for that to happen.'

'Now therein, Andy,' DI Sally Speckle said, 'could be the real motive.'

* * *

'Ms Mayhew,' DC Charlie Johnson called out, after his third knock on the door of Judy Mayhew's flat, and for the second time added, 'Police.' When no response was forth-coming, he stepped aside for uniform to break in.

'Oi! Wha'cha think yer doin'?'

'And you are?' Johnson enquired, of the

angry woman clattering up the stairs.

'Me name's Kitty Crook, if you must know,' she stated brazenly. 'Now what's goin' on?'

'We've made several unsuccessful attempts to contact Ms Mayhew,' Johnson explained. 'We thought that she might be ill and need our help.'

'Oh, yeah,' said Kitty Crook sceptically. 'Pull the other one. Anyway, Judy is feelin' a bit under the weather and she ain't here. She's with me, ain't she?'

'And where would that be?' Johnson enquired.

'Across the street.'

'Lead the way then.'

'I don't know if Judy will want to see you lot, do I?'

'Ever heard of obstructing the police, Ms Crook?' Johnson said, hating coming the heavy but also not of a mind to mess about.

'A bloody police state,' Crook complained, clattering back down the stairs on needle thin stiletto heels. 'That's what I've been sayin'. We're livin' in a police state. I'd write to my MP, if I could write and he could read.' Her rant lasted all the way to her flat, informing Mayhew as she entered, 'Ain't none of my doin', Judy. I told 'em, I said, Judy might not want to see you lot. But it's a police state, ain't it?'

'It's all right, Kitty,' said Judy Mayhew, seated at a rickety kitchen table, sipping a cup of instant soup, the bruises on her face a dirty yellow. 'A bloke who thought I should be punished for damning his soul,' she said, by way of explanation.

'Did you report the assault to the police?' Johnson asked, sympathetically.

'Don't be daft!' Crook scoffed. 'It could've been a copper, done it, couldn't it? Anyway, what would you lot do about it?'

'What is it you want to talk to me about?' Mayhew asked.

'We're enquiring about a man called Jack Ansome, used to do odd jobs at the Old Mill.'

'I know what Jack used to do. What about him?'

'Where we might find him, Ms Mayhew.'

'Through a medium, maybe,' Mayhew said. 'Jack Ansome's dead. A couple of weeks ago.'

'Are you sure?' Johnson checked.

'Yes. Besides the undertaker and a half-pissed vicar, I was the only one at his funeral. He turned up on my patch a week before he died, pretty far gone. Went into hospital a couple of days later.' Judy Mayhew laughed sadly. 'Jack could be a thorny customer, a spoiled Bible-basher with more hang-ups than a beard has hairs, but I was glad that in the end he came to me for help.'

'Thank you,' Johnson said. 'Sorry for troubling you.'

'A bloody police state, that's what it is,' said Kitty Crook, slamming the door of the flat shut, fit to rattle the rafters.

★ ★ ★

Professor Stanley, the Medical Director at Loston Mental Hospital, was none too pleased to see Speckle and Lukeson back.

'I can, of course, understand your concerns, Professor,' Speckle said. 'But it's vital that we try to discover who took the patient's dressing-gown from the hydrotherapy unit. And I think James can point the finger.'

'It must have been a shock arriving home to find a body in your house.'

'It was,' Speckle said.

The newspapers were full of sensational headlines and reports that, where facts were not available, were based on speculation. Anything to sell copies.

'I'll arrange for the group to be assembled, Inspector. But, as before, I shall be the sole arbiter of when the interview should end. Agreed?'

'Agreed. But I'd like to speak to James alone.'

'Out of the question,' Stanley stated with

uncompromising bluntness. 'There are dangers in James being interviewed as part of a group, although the group gives a sense of security and familiarity which is very important, like a family. The effect of being separated from the group and being isolated could have unforseen consequences, and I will not take that risk.'

'Group or nothing, Inspector.'

'The group it is then, Professor.'

'Do you honestly think that this killer could be connected with the hospital?'

'At the moment we're ruling nothing out or in,' Speckle replied, striking a cautious note. 'There is one other matter — '

'There always is with the police.'

'I believe that you have a patient by the name of Mary Alcott here? A word with her — '

'Would be absolutely useless,' Stanley interjected. 'She hasn't uttered a single word since she was admitted to psychiatric care many years ago. It's my belief that she's incurably catatonic, Inspector. She has only ever had one visitor, and all he does is sit there, doting on her, telling her over and over that he stills loves her. Can't understand why he keeps punishing himself. It's all quite hopeless.'

'Do you know who this man is, Professor?'

'Off hand, I can't recall his name. But Loston General should be able to help you there, Sergeant.'

'Loston General?'

'Yes. He's a nurse there. Comes here to escort patients who need treatment.'

'A *male* nurse?'

Stanley's chuckle was a wry one. 'Unless he's a very good drag artiste, Inspector.'

'Was he the nurse who helped to restore order in the hydrotherapy unit when the disturbance broke out?'

'Well, he tried, of course. But Jack, the patient who threw a tantrum, wouldn't have him around. So he had to leave. Can't understand why, because Jack and he used to be pretty chummy.'

'Does Jack go to Loston General for treatment?'

'Yes.'

'The renal clinic?'

'Yes. How did you know?'

'An educated guess, Professor.'

'Blake,' Stanley said, tapping his forehead. 'That's his name, Inspector.'

'Can I see James now?' she enquired urgently. 'Alone,' she pleaded. 'It's vitally important, Professor.' And when Stanley hesitated. 'I have just one question to ask him.'

'Pray he'll be in a co-operative mood, Andy,' she said, again trying to keep pace with Stanley's loping stride.

★ ★ ★

James looked moody. Speckle's hopes took a set back.

'Hello, James,' she said, friendly, but not over friendly. She did not want James to think he was being cajoled. She suspected that his personality was such that he would reject any approach he thought was fawning or outright nonsense. 'You remember me, don't you?' He did not give any hint that he did. 'Can I ask you one simple question, James?'

James gave no encouragement. However, neither did he reject the proposition out of hand. 'Shall I take that as a yes, then?'

He nodded.

'Thank you. Who stole your dressing-gown, James?'

James looked beyond Speckle at some distant point, completely uninterested in her and her question. There was nothing she could do. She was tempted to ask if it was Nurse Blake, but she was only too aware that later if the case came to court, Blake would stand a very good chance of having the case thrown out, if the mainstay of identification

253

was a mentally disturbed patient who had been led by a police officer.

'Thank you anyway James,' Speckle said pleasantly.

She was at the door when James said, clear as a bell, 'Nurse Blake, Inspector. He took my dressing-gown.'

Speckle thanked James again.

'I'd like it if you called again sometime,' he said.

'I shall,' Sally Speckle promised, and meant it.

James's smile was filled with the sadness of a life which had taken a cruel turn; a life the promise of which had been snatched away by the demons who had invaded his head.

Clipping along the hall, Speckle explained to Lukeson, 'When I arrested Mary Alcott there was a young man about Alcott's age, her boyfriend, I think. He called me a Nazi cow and promised to get even with me one day. How could I have forgotten!'

'It's easy,' Lukeson said. 'If you get threats slung at you almost every day, you just never expect them to be acted on.'

She punched out DC Helen Rochester's mobile number.

'Helen, are you at Loston General yet? Good. We're looking for a Nurse Blake — a male nurse. I think he's Fred . . . Yes, Helen,

254

we're pre-conditioned to think of a nurses as female. Andy and I will be with you in about ten minutes.'

★ ★ ★

Helen Rochester went through the doors marked: RENAL CLINIC.

'Nurse Blake?' The head nurse, whose name tag identified her as Angela Crumb, looked closely and concernedly at Rochester's warrant card. 'Not here I'm afraid. He called in sick.'

'I need Blake's address.'

'Is Nurse Blake in some kind of trouble? He's been acting a bit strange of late.'

That's a bloody understatement, Rochester thought.

'The address, please,' Rochester demanded, much to the annoyance of Head Nurse Crumb.

'I'm afraid that we don't hand out addresses willy-nilly, Officer.'

'You're obstructing the police, Nurse Crumb. And that can have very serious consequences.'

Losing her bottle, Crumb mumbled, 'Well I don't want to do that, of course. 60 Claremont Street. Flat nine.' And, by way of explantion, 'It was my flat before I was promoted. With an increase in salary, I moved out. Bought my own house. But he's not home.'

255

'How do you know that?'

'I phoned. I lost the keys to my front door, and I was hoping that he'd open it for me, without doing any damage. Someone's always losing or mislaying keys, even here at the hospital. So we call on Nurse Blake to help out. He's a wizard with locks of all shapes and sizes.'

'You used to have a patient, Claire Shaw . . .'

'Yes. She changed to the Lintree Clinic,' she added a little huffily.

'Friendly with Blake, was she?'

'Yes. Unprofessional, really. Best to keep everything on a business footing. But, of course, patients here are longterm and a rapport with staff is sometimes inevitable.'

Moments later, DI Sally Speckle received Helen Rochester's report, and was instructed to head straight for Claremont Street.

★ ★ ★

The clack of the woman's heels came along the tiled hall. Fred put his eye to the crack in the partially open sitting-room door as she passed on, but a little further along the hall she paused and glanced back at the open door, curiously, Fred recalled that the door had been closed when he had arrived. She

256

had obviously remembered that it had been, obsessive cow. She would have probably noticed a new speck of dust in a cellar. She turned and came back. Fred pressed back against the wall behind the door. Would she just shut the door? Or would she come into the room? Seeing himself in the mirror over the fireplace, Fred saw a present and sudden danger. Coming to the door, she would have to see him in the mirror. And if he tried to move further along the wall, she might see or sense him. And even if he were successful in moving, he would have distanced himself from the room's entrance. And should she come into the room, that gap could give her the chance to react. She was a very fit woman. She might not be easily overcome. And even if she screamed, there was the chance that some- one would come to investigate.

There was one other option open to him, and that was to pounce and gain the advantage of surprise.

★ ★ ★

The door of flat nine, 60 Claremont Street provided little resistance to the uniformed officers. The stench from the room hit them full on.

'The bloody place is a tip,' said the first

uniformed officer into the flat.

Heaps of filthy clothing, including several items of soiled underwear littered the floor and sofa. Partially eaten take-aways were tossed at random about the place. A rat, nibbling on a discarded scrap fled through the filth, squealing in protest at the intrusion. Near Speckle's foot, some discarded under-pants moved, before another rat broke from cover and scurried after the other one. She leaped back into Andy Lukeson's arms.

He grinned.

'It's one way to get the girl,' he said.

Sally Speckle found herself thinking that another time, and she might remain right where she was for longer than she could now. 'I want every crawling inch of this place gone over,' she ordered, somewhat annoyed by Lukeson's even wider grin, and wondering if he had sensed her reluctance to disengage.

The uniformed officers exchanged concerned glances.

'We're not togged out, ma'am,' said one of the PCs.

'This is no time for squeamishness,' Speckle stated, and led by example. 'I think Blake alias Fred is on the sick because he's on to his next victim, and I'm hoping that somewhere in this sewer there's a scrap of information that will prevent another murder.'

258

Fred was ready to spring when the top copper's mobile rang. 'Mulgrave,' she answered crossly. Mulgrave. Fred recalled reading about her in the *Loston Echo*. The newly appointed Assistant Chief Constable. He smiled. It would be a short-term appointment. She sniffed the air and looked towards the kitchen. 'I'll phone you back, Frank.' She hurried into the kitchen and saw that the microwave was switched on. Shocked, she switched it off. Was she losing it? Leaving the microwave switched on? But she hadn't used the microwave. Something was cooking. Intrigued, she opened the door of the microwave and staggered back, intrigue replaced by shuddering fear and revulsion. She might have been sick, had she had time to, but the prick of a hypodermic needle at her throat froze her.

'Take it nice and easy now,' Blake whispered in Alice Mulgrave's ear, rubbing against her.

Looking down, she thought: White shoes. How ridiculously silly for a man's footwear.

CS Frank 'Sermon' Doyle checked his watch. 'Don't take too long,' he grumbled. 'I'm dead on my feet.' The phone rang. 'That was quick, ma'am,' he answered. Then: 'Speckle?'

★ ★ ★

'Drop the mobile on the floor,' Blake said. Mulgrave dropped the phone she was holding. He stamped on it. 'Don't want to be interrupted, do we? Upstairs.' As he passed the phone in the hall, he ripped it from its connection. 'You know, this is really going to piss off DI Sally Speckle big time.' Mulgrave glimpsed her assailant in a hall mirror, and she understood the shoes — Fred, because she was certain that's who he was, was wearing a nurse's uniform.

As he turned into her bedroom, Mulgrave felt the nip of the needle pierce her skin and a moment later her world spun out of control. Her muzzy thought was: Fred is a male nurse. That would be good to know. Then, as a black cloak began to enclose her, Alice Mulgrave knew that, though the information would be vital in nailing Fred, it would not matter because the dead could not speak.

She felt incredibly sad.

★ ★ ★

'We've turned over every inch of the kip,' Lukeson said, to a frowning Speckle, and added pointedly, 'Twice.'

'There's got to be something of use here, Andy.'

Frank Doyle entered the flat, and stopped dead in his tracks. 'Mother of Moses,' he exclaimed, looking around, his hand going to his mouth. 'A pigsty would be a four-star hotel compared to this bug-infested dump.'

'You're just in time, sir,' Lukeson said.

'Am I? For what?'

'To join in, sir.' The sergeant's grin was mischievous.

'Join in?' Doyle's eyes lit with alarm. 'You mean . . . ?'

'It's this curb on overtime, sir,' Lukeson said. 'Leaves us short-handed.'

'Remind me to bust your balls later, Sergeant,' the CS growled in an undertone, as he went past Andy Lukeson.

'Ma'am.' All eyes went to the PC holding up a section of a pizza carton with his fingertips. 'Might mean nothing, but there's a street name scribbled on this.' He held it up to the light from the window. 'Looks like Crescent Road.'

'Crescent Road!'

All eyes now switched to Frank Doyle.

'That's where our shiny new Assistant

Chief Constable has taken up residence.'
'Do you know where, sir?' Speckle asked.
'In my brother-in-law's house,' Doyle said.

★   ★   ★

Muzzily, Alice Mulgrave felt the bite of the binding on her ankles as Blake tightened the bonds. Her hands had already been tied to the bedposts. She had a hazy sense of being cold, colder than she should be. Leaning over her, as if examining a lab specimen, Blake hovered in a fog. He seemed so far away, much too distant to be a threat to her, and yet she instinctively knew that he was.

He had given her a mild sedative to make her compliant. In a short while it would wear off, she would see her nakedness and be shocked, and her shock would be all the greater when a full realization of what lay ahead of her struck home.

He had been surprised and pleased when he had stripped her, by the firmness of her body. He had expected some sagging, some disgusting loose flesh, but there was none. Alice Mulgrave was a woman who took good care of herself, exercised regularly and obviously watched what she ate — as he had, before that bitch Speckle had arrested Mary and she was sectioned. After that he had let himself go, reasoning that there was little point in keeping himself fit and healthy, because he could never imagine himself falling in love with another woman. Although he had briefly been drawn to Claire Shaw, there really would never be a woman who could come anywhere near Mary Alcott's perfection. A bit of a temper, had Mary, but she had never once been cross with him — with him she had been soft and gentle and infinitely loving. And Speckle had taken Mary from him.

When it had been decided that she would never really get better, she had been sent to Loston Mental Hospital where her family could visit her. Only they upped and left for Devon, leaving Mary all alone. That's when he had transferred to Loston General Hospital, to be close to her. Mary had always wanted to be a nurse, so when she had been sectioned and all chance of her ever fulfilling her ambition had gone, he had become a nurse, figuring that through him Mary would be a nurse by proxy.

'You can blame your precious DI Speckle for this, you know,' he said angrily. He gave an effeminate twirl. 'Nothing like the caring profession to open all doors. And if that fails, having had a stepfather who was a locksmith helps.'

Arriving quietly in Crescent Road ten minutes later, everyone obeying Speckle's 'no sirens,' approach, Lukeson said, 'If Blake is in the house, he'll have nothing to lose. He'll be a cornered animal and very dangerous.'

Chief Superintendent Doyle dangled a key ring. 'If Mulgrave hasn't had the locks changed, and I can't see any reason why she would have had, these should work. My brother-in-law left spare keys with me to keep an eye on the house until it was rented.'

The front door opened easily and sound-lessly, and Sally Speckle stepped quickly into the hall with Andy Lukeson, just as an ancient motor-scooter rattled past. She closed the door and listened. The stillness of the house was intense.

Upstairs, Blake paused, listened, ears cocked and alert. Was he imagining that he had heard traffic go past? A motor-scooter? How could that be? He had been in the house for over three hours now, and he had not heard any traffic go past. The old Victorian pile was built like a fortress. He crossed to the bedroom door and slowly opened it.

Lukeson was first to react. He pulled Speckle into the nearest room, just as Blake popped his head out of the open bedroom door. He came to the head of the stairs and looked down into the hall and waited. Satisfied that his imagination had played a trick on him, he returned to the bedroom and closed the door.

Andy Lukeson and Sally Speckle came from the sitting-room, and were on their way upstairs when the lock on the bedroom door was turned. On reaching the landing, Lukeson took a couple of steps back and charged the door, hoping that one shoulder charge would be enough to shift it. The door slammed back against the wall, sending a picture crashing to the floor; its glass shattered, sunlight through the bedroom window glinting on the shards as they spun across the polished floorboards. Alice Mulgrave was on the bed, Blake leaning over her. Lukeson continued his charge and thudded into Blake, who spun backwards out of control towards the window behind him. Seeing the danger, Andy Lukeson clutched at Blake, but while the impact had slowed him, it had accelerated Blake's backwards spiral and Lukeson's purchase on him was token. Blake crashed through the old sash window. His scream lasted only seconds before it was lost in the thud of his contact with the ground below. Looking down, and seeing Blake's oddly angled neck, one back for Cromwell, he thought, with a rapidly expanding pool of blood spreading out from under his head, Lukeson said, 'Roast in hell, you sick bastard!'

* * *

'That's it,' Doyle said, pouring the last drops of champagne into Sally Speckle's glass.

'How is our new ACC?' Charlie Johnson enquired.

'Still a bit groggy, but no permanent damage,' Doyle said. 'Looking forward to seeing you lot when she's on her feet again.'

There was a knock on the office door, and immediately a man's head appeared.

'DCI Amber,' he announced, arrogantly stepping into Doyle's office, casting a jaundiced eye at a group of officers who were obviously tipsy, 'DI Benson and DS Sharer.' He pointed to a man and a woman following him in. 'Regional Crime Squad.'

'You lot are too late,' Doyle said, smugly. 'Case solved.' CS Frank 'Sermon' Doyle raised his glass. 'Cheers. And bloody well done everyone!'

'A word, sir,' Johnson said, hanging back.

'If it's about your transfer, Johnson,' the CS said. 'It'll take effect from Monday week.'

'Mind if I forget the whole thing, sir?' Johnson said.

'If that's what you want.'

'It is, sir.'

'Mind if I ask why you changed your mind?'

'I think that now, after DI Speckle was overruled by Alice Mulgrave, she'll have a better understanding of how I felt when she appointed Rochester over me when Andy Lukeson was away on that course. So I reckon that that makes it all water under the bridge, sir. You might say that she swallowed the medicine and got on with it.'

'Sally Speckle is a strong-willed woman, Charlie,' Doyle said. 'In the future she might act in a manner that doesn't meet with your approval again.'

'If that happens, I think the difference the next time round will be that I'll know she acted out of conviction, sir.'

'A fine DI, Sally Speckle,' Doyle said.

'That she is,' DC Charlie Johnson agreed. He looked to Sally Speckle. 'That she is, sir.'

DS Andy Lukeson popped his head back in the office, 'Mrs Madge Scott ring a bell, Charlie?'

'Yes, Sarge. She's the elderly woman Benny

Frederics robbed. But she can't or won't identify him. The no-good bastard even robbed the small change in her purse.'

'That was the mistake he made, Charlie,' Lukeson said. 'He dropped a twenty pence coin. Rolled under a couch. Left a pair of fingerprints, one either side, thumb and first finger, that's a perfect match for prints from a drunk and disorderly for which Frederics was arrested two years ago.'

'You've got your man, Charlie, boyo!'

We do hope that you have enjoyed reading this large print book.

Did you know that all of our titles are available for purchase?

We publish a wide range of high quality large print books including:
Romances, Mysteries, Classics
General Fiction
Non Fiction and Westerns

Special interest titles available in large print are:
The Little Oxford Dictionary
Music Book
Song Book
Hymn Book
Service Book

Also available from us courtesy of Oxford University Press:
Young Readers' Dictionary
(large print edition)
Young Readers' Thesaurus
(large print edition)

For further information or a free brochure, please contact us at:
Ulverscroft Large Print Books Ltd.,
The Green, Bradgate Road, Anstey,
Leicester, LE7 7FU, England.
Tel: (00 44) **0116 236 4325**
Fax: (00 44) **0116 234 0205**

Other titles published by
The House of Ulverscroft:

REMAINS FOUND

J. A. O'Brien

Two children find a woman's body which is identified first by a friend called Ruby Cox, as Diane Shaft, and later by another friend, Aiden Brooks, as Cecily Staunton. Why did the dead woman have two names? DI Sally Speckle's problems start when Cox vanishes from Loston police station. Then Brooks, claiming he's a clairvoyant, accurately pinpoints the location of where the body was discovered. Does this mean that Brooks is the killer? But as the investigation gets increasingly complicated by troubles far closer to home, followed by another murder, Sally finds she has more suspects than she wants . . .

OLD BONES

J. A. O'Brien

When skeletal remains of a female are found in Thatcher's Lot, Loston CID is involved and DI Sally Speckle and her team investigate. The remains have been in the ground for five years — disturbingly, there were several women who went missing around that time. The missing women come from divergent backgrounds, but the skull has evidence of expensive dental care which Sally hopes will help to identify the remains. However, due to DC Helen Rochester's astuteness, the other women come into focus and unlikely suspects emerge. Now it starts to become a murder investigation within a murder investigation . . .

PICK UP

J. A. O'Brien

Jack Carver is experiencing the most horrible of all nightmares: being an innocent man who is the prime suspect in the brutal murder of two women. Forensic evidence is found at both crime scenes, which implicates Carver. And when the police request that he should come forward, he goes on the run instead. He is finally apprehended, but an incident from Carver's past shakes his absolute certainty that he is not the killer. Then he is charged with murder. Can DS Andy Lukeson prove his innocence when a chance incident prompts him to reassess the case?

BURIAL

Neil Cross

Nathan has never been able to forget the worst night of his life: the party that led to the sudden, shocking death of a young woman. Only he and Bob, an untrustworthy old acquaintance, know what really happened and they have resolved to keep it that way. But when, years later, Bob appears at Nathan's door with terrifying news, old wounds are reopened, threatening to tear Nathan's world apart. Because Nathan has his own secrets now. Secrets that could destroy everything he has fought to build. And maybe Bob doesn't realise just how far Nathan will go to protect them . . .

DEADLIER THAN THE SWORD

Jean Rowden

Constable 'Thorny' Deepbriar anticipates a peaceful interlude as Minecliff prepares for its summer fete. However, following an incident involving an illegal mantrap, there is a suspicious death on the arterial road, and suddenly he has more than enough work. Adding to his troubles, Deepbriar's childhood friend has returned home with his fiancee to plan their wedding, unaware that the village is harbouring dark secrets . . . With someone causing mayhem on the local byways, and malicious letters, written anonymously, to members of Minecliff's community, the constable faces a serious challenge to his detection skills, and ultimately, a threat to his own life . . .

1	21	41	61	81	101	121	141	161	181
2	22	42	62	82	102	122	142	162	182
3	23	43	63	83	103	123	143	163	183
4	24	44	64	84	104	124	144	164	184
5	25	45	65	85	105	125	145	165	185
6	26	46	66	86	106	126	146	166	186
7	27	47	67	87	107	127	147	167	187
8	28	48	68	88	108	128	148	168	188
9	29	49	69	89	109	129	149	169	189
10	30	50	70	90	110	130	150	170	190
11	31	51	71	91	111	131	151	171	191
12	32	52	72	92	112	132	152	172	192
13	33	53	73	93	113	133	153	173	193
14	34	54	74	94	114	134	154	174	194
15	35	55	75	95	115	135	155	175	195
16	36	56	76	96	116	136	156	176	196
17	37	57	77	97	117	137	157	177	197
18	38	58	78	98	118	138	158	178	198
19	39	59	79	99	119	139	159	179	199
20	40	60	80	100	120	140	160	180	200

201	216	231	246	261	276	291	306	321	336
202	217	232	247	262	277	292	307	322	337
203	218	233	248	263	278	293	308	323	338
204	219	234	249	264	279	294	309	324	339
205	220	235	250	265	280	295	310	325	340
206	221	236	251	266	281	296	311	326	341
207	222	237	252	267	282	297	312	327	342
208	223	238	253	268	283	298	313	328	343
209	224	239	254	269	284	299	314	329	344
210	225	240	255	270	285	300	315	330	345
211	226	241	256	271	286	301	316	331	346
212	227	242	257	272	287	302	317	332	347
213	228	243	258	273	288	303	318	333	348
214	229	244	259	274	289	304	319	334	349
215	230	245	260	275	290	305	320	335	350